THE ART OF WEARING A TRENCH COAT

THE
ART OF
WEARING A
TRENCH COAT

Stories

Sergi Pàmies

Translated from the Catalan by
Adrian Nathan West

OTHER PRESS
NEW YORK

LLLL institut
ramon llull

The translation of this novel was made possible thanks to the
support of the Institut Ramon Llull.

Production editor: Yvonne E. Cárdenas
Text designer: Jennifer Daddio / Bookmark Design & Media Inc.
This book was set in Horley Old Style
by Alpha Design & Composition of Pittsfield, NH

1 3 5 7 8 10 8 6 4 2

Library of Congress Cataloging-in-Publication Data
Names: Pàmies, Sergi, 1960- author. | West, Adrian Nathan, translator.
Title: The art of wearing a trench coat : stories / Sergi Pàmies ; translated from the
Catalan by Adrian Nathan West.
Description: New York : Other Press, [2021] | Originally published in Catalan as
L'art de portar gavardina in 2018 by Quaderns Crema, Barcelona.
Identifiers: LCCN 2020029876 (print) | LCCN 2020029877 (ebook) |
ISBN 9781635420784 (paperback) | ISBN 9781635420791 (ebook)
Subjects: LCSH: Pàmies, Sergi, 1960—Translations into English.
Classification: LCC PC3942.26.A52 A6 2021 (print) | LCC PC3942.26.A52 (ebook) |
DDC 849/.9354—dc23
LC record available at https://lccn.loc.gov/2020029876
LC ebook record available at https://lccn.loc.gov/2020029877

CONTENTS

ECLIPSE

We've met next to a hotel pool. As yet there is not a body
floating in it. It's the birthday—the fiftieth—of a well-
known radio announcer. The nearly two hundred guests
were chosen from among family members, friends, and
work colleagues. The view overlooks seven miles of
beachfront in the form of a crescent moon, a horizon that
weaves together all the colors of the dusk, and a procession of airplanes making their way toward the airport in
orderly succession. A common friend has introduced us, a
woman who insists we'll want to get to know each other.
During the two perfunctory kisses on the cheek, each of
us detects in the other the same blend of bashfulness and
tension. Perhaps because we don't want to disappoint this
friend in common, our first look is one of resignation, as
if we had agreed wordlessly to put an end to this ordeal as
soon as possible. The mutual scrutiny persists until we

get in sync. Our friend has left us high and dry. Now it depends on us whether or not the conversation drowns in the pool. We do what we can. You with a deference I'm grateful for. Me with a gracelessness made worse through years of lethargy. We cycle through effervescent questions and answers until my resources run dry and I propose we get a drink from the bar. You order cava, I order wine; I know myself, and I suppress the temptation to come up with some theory as to why. We toast to the honoree, who thanks us and announces that in a few months, he'll be appearing in a play. We don't clap, because we have glasses in our hands, and we ask each other how he will manage to balance these performances with the six hours a day he spends on the radio. "He'll give up sleeping," you conclude, with unqualified common sense. At that instant, I do what I had not dared to do before: instead of seeing you and hearing you, I look and listen. The unease I feel when socializing does not keep me from noticing the harmony between the color of your eyes and the intro-verted vibrancy of your stare, the attention you seem to pay to your hair and the gentleness in your smile. Our questions are no longer effervescent, and, even though we're talking about work, I have the sense that we're pick-ing up a conversation begun some time back. Differences between a moment ago and now: a moment ago, I didn't mind coming across as a misanthrope, and now I would do anything to avoid it. I calculate that no more than ten minutes have passed since we were introduced, and you've had time to tell me you graduated with a degree in humanities (with a thesis on the function of landscape in the works of Mary Shelley and Edgar Allan Poe) and that you have some kind of business deal in the works. I arrange, in descending order, like the planes making their way to the airport, the questions I would like to ask you. Like a control tower, I register your eyes, which project a series of coded signals I wish I were able to decipher. I take an unusually long sip of wine. A sommelier would detect in it notes of disorientation, an aftertaste of panic, and a hint of citrus: the adrenaline of volatile expectations. I am no longer pretending to have a conversation: I am having one. And this entails listening more than speaking, and not rushing and not asking why you studied humanities or what sense of irony led you to pick Shelley and Poe. But just as I prepare to address you at greater length, to enhance the impression I must be giving, the jubilant host picks the microphone back up and invites us all to continue the party on the twenty-sixth floor of the hotel, at a dance club reserved for the occasion. Immediately, the guests start filing out. A man appears next to you, still of an age and appearance that permit him to call himself young, familiar in the way a brother is rather than a friend, and he encourages—even urges—you to go along with him. Now it hits me that I don't know a thing about you. Do you have children? Are

you divorced, too? Did you come alone? I don't even
know how old you are, though I'd say you are the kind of
person whose looks are a faithful indication of their age. I
take a step back and accept, with the good sportsmanship
of someone never in the running, that this pro forma
ritual is now at an end. We don't say goodbye. I'd like to
believe this is because we think the party is informal
enough that more comings and goings are in the offing.
You walk off with your brother/friend while I say hi to
other guests and force myself to analyze our meeting
pragmatically: most likely you didn't come alone; most
likely you're married. The attendees, many of them couples, are waiting for the elevators to arrive. To go up—ten
seconds of supersonic ascent—we were required to put on
an orange wristband (with access to the open bar)
stamped with a circle with the word *eclipse* inside. The
last time I wore a wristband was at the hospital, I remember. After an attack of lipothymia accompanied by amnesia, they took me in and gave me a diagnosis more a
disappointment than a relief: stress. From the windows of
the twenty-sixth floor, the panorama improves. The ver-
tical and horizontal grandeur of the landscape seems
heightened by an unusual perspective on the pool. Despite the distance, which reduces its proportions to those
of an architectural model, I would swear there is a body,
perfectly illuminated, floating on the surface of the water.
I say nothing, because I might be hallucinating, and enter

the dance club. I avoid the booming speakers and try to participate in conversations about two omnipresent topics: Twitter and Catalan independence. When I talk, I have the feeling no one hears me. I don't look around for you so it won't seem I'm trying to force an ostensibly chance meeting of the eyes. As always, I envy the dissolute aplomb of the people out on the dance floor. Pleased, the host is talking with a friend, a famed musician, who volunteered to play disc jockey and whose perfect repertory is neither too nostalgic nor too modern. I order a gin and tonic and they serve it to me with the proportions reversed. I grab it, impatient to see how long the mix of alcohol and the new medications I've been prescribed will take to strike me down. The effect is immediate. The minutes heap up in my mind, annihilate the most active of the neurons, and make me feel more circumspect than normal. This may be why, when friends who live close to home offer to give me a lift in their car, I accept, even knowing I'll regret leaving without saying anything to you. I take leave of the radio announcer with a cordial handshake, and when we reach the parking garage, I get a message from him: "Sorry you didn't have fun. But thanks for coming. I mean it. Cheers!" I wonder how he diagnosed my mood, which I myself wasn't aware of. By now, the friends who offered me a ride are struggling with the machine in the parking garage, which keeps spitting out a corporate credit card meant to be accepted in any and all situations. They try again and again, in an ever-deepening rage, until, to ease matters, I slide in a banknote, which the machine devours hungrily. "Machines prefer cash to credit," I affirm, as if it's some kind of neoliberal maxim. We get into the car and leave the hotel via a diabolically curvy ramp. More than squeal, the tires scream. We have to stop near the entrance because, between two police cars, paramedics in reflective vests are loading a corpse covered with an emergency blanket into an ambulance. The stretcher passes close enough for us to see a wet sleeve and a dangling arm—plus wristband—the loafers of the deceased, identical to my own, and, lit bright by the sirens, the gnawed nails on the hand and a Swatch, which, like mine, tells the time from three hours ago. I imagine our common friend calling you tomorrow to say: "You know that guy I introduced you to? They found him drowned in the pool." The police order us to take a detour through neighborhoods I didn't know existed. Through the car's tinted windows, the city looks like the capital of a country of vampires who feed not on blood but on noise and euphoria. The people move in groups, in slow motion, and those not busy tapping their cell phone screens wave at us at the zebra crossings and none of us respects the color of the traffic lights. I suspect that this hallucinatory impression is a flight strategy to avoid admitting that, against medical advice, I am thinking of you more than I can bear to. And I also have

the sense that those minutes we were together are insuffi-
cient to afford me any precision when eventually I try to
recollect you. And so, before it gets too late, I scan your
eyes, your hair, and the vertices of your smile in my
mind. It's a smile that portends warm peals of laughter I
would love to share, were I not dead and laid out on a
stretcher in an ambulance.

OUTLINE OF A LECTURE FOR A HYPOTHETICAL CONFERENCE OF DIVORCEES

.1.

Couples who divorce should wait neither for the decline
into boredom nor for the temptation to deceive. At the
moment of plenty, when love is borne forward by enthusiasm and shared affinities, both parties should be generous enough to leave things be and agree, with the feeling
of a job well done, on a finale that will not dishonor the
time they shared. This would save them the pain of
giving up and the trial of seeing their feelings for what
they are rather than as a pretext for the transformation of
affection into repulsion or indifference. Like elite athletes,
who realize it as soon as they reach the end of their prime,

lovers should have the loyalty and courage to protect
each other. Doing so would mean consideration for that
respect for freedom that languishes and finally rots when
a relationship stretches on through stubbornness alone.
It's not true that the erosion is imperceptible. Long before
the point of festering, it makes itself known through details couples notice but refuse to acknowledge, because
inertia has hobbled their capacity for decision-making
or because they try to believe better days are on the way.
Though it doesn't seem so, these postponements can be
fruitful. The proof is how frequently they yield offspring
and shared moments that transform us so that, when
we try to go back to what we were, we realize feelings
evolve faster than the people who experience them. This
discrepancy produces misunderstandings and multiplies
opportunities to ignore what is evident. A sense of guilt
heightens the inevitable ending's mediocrity. This is why,
for the first seconds of the breakup proper, my reaction
reveals a desire to live up not to our last few years together, but to the whole of our shared history. Once more,
I visualize the scene, which probably resembles scenes
many of you have lived through yourselves. She tells me
I've been expecting her to *tell me* for a long time. That
we need to talk. That she no longer loves me. That she's
met someone. That they're seeing each other. First I feel
hot and ashamed. The two sensations are contradictory,
unexpected, cruel. I check: the heat is more emotional

than physical. The shame, on the other hand, makes my muscles tense and dynamites the scaffolding of normalcy we've taken refuge behind without fully grasping all the risks involved. I don't need to think to realize the change we've just initiated has countless consequences, but no way back. Sorrow isn't long in coming, and, with a sense of priority that surprises even me, I lay down a condition: no self-deceptions. If I already had a intuition, I can't pretend this came out of nowhere. To avoid unnecessary difficulties, I put principle before emotion. The gulf between us is epitomized in the way she crosses her arms and looks down, weak from overdoing herself. I pinpoint the origin of my shame: my recognition that the fact that I love her now means nothing to her, that even the comfort of a companion more willing than able no longer matters. We're in the kitchen, which has always seemed like the ideal terrain for truth-telling. In the kitchen, privacy is relative. You hear the dryers beeping, the whir of the washers in the inner courtyard, and the refrigerator's cyclothymic hum plays the role of fair-minded mediator. I look at her and, without saying so, thank her for what I've reproached her for before: resorting to unfathomable silence until everything gets summed up in a categorical message followed—I always have the impression with her that each abyss leads to a new one—by another silence. This time, appearances don't deceive. The fluorescent lights harden our expressions and defuse the temptation to cry. We only split up five minutes ago, and already, it feels like two years. Now I can admit it: subconsciously, I had prepared myself to reach this point. I've made it through all the training phases, the most exasperating ones and the most promising. And I'm amazed at the quantity of resources I realize I possess. I'm also anxious to see how much my training will help me avoid paroxysms of reproach and rancor. I could turn this breakup into an act that will lend coherence to all we've lived through without debasing us more than we've debased ourselves by staying captive to a now-obsolete respect. When we first knew each other, we were improvising. And so it hits me that in this loveless phase we've just inaugurated, we'll have to be stricter and avoid letting random fits of spontaneity blind us. And the conviction that there will be much more love in this breakup than in the decline that preceded it has an analgesic effect; I don't know why.

.2.

We didn't make a good couple. We both knew it, but we had the good taste not to bring it up. When two people meet and feel attracted to each other, the story that commemorates their first meeting is usually benign. But in our case, the seduction wasn't bilateral. For years, I had been prepared to let myself be seduced, but I never imagined I'd be lucky enough to be abducted—this is the verb that best describes what happened—by a person like her. Analyzing things with a certain retrospective rigor, it strikes me that everything was the consequence of a prior reality that I would never know. That she was interested in me more for reasons related to circumstances in her past—dominoes lined up behind me—than for my own seductive endowments. Fortunately or unfortunately, you see this only later, not while it's actually happening. We met at a party and had something strange in common, and it left me with the impression that I'd won the lottery or was the dupe of some perverse wager. At the time, the novelty of it restrained my euphoria, and I assumed the experience would be as unrepeatable as it had been fleeting. The proof is, on the day after the numerous days that memory has compressed into one, when I left home suffused with the ecstasy of the chosen—dancing in the street, imitating a scene from a perfume ad—I never thought there was the least possibility we would meet again. It's not polite to say it, but at the moment of affiliation, bonding, or what have you, there are signs a person should never lose sight of. Generally speaking, a union of two people evinces a clear disparity in beauty, status, or intelligence. I fell short in all three, and might only have matched her in good humor (the good humor I possessed back then, that is), in my eagerness to live to the fullest the hours of contentment fate had granted me... and in

my willingness to know how to say goodbye to them
when the time came. That's why I was so surprised she
wanted to see me again. And even more when, weeks
later, we had already become inseparable (as I write, I
notice the vulnerability of this adjective). I concentrated
on living this requited love with the same intensity I'd
devoted to other, unrequited loves in the past. Returning
to the image of the lottery: maybe the winner is perfectly
aware of the perils lying in wait for him but chooses con-
sciously to proceed for no other reason than to see what
unimaginable catastrophe the privilege of winning will
bring him. These are the years I like to remember best.
They have the right measure of surprise and variety and
include lots of travel and, at least on my part, a permanent state of gratitude. Said otherwise: even if I managed
to believe love could be reciprocal, I also understood that,
from the scientific perspective, it was unlikely that someone like her would fall in love with someone like me. I'm
not saying this from false modesty, or to play the victim.
On the contrary. Precisely because I am vain, I chose to
draw my love out to the maximum, trusting I would find
a way to sustain it. But the natural transition from exceptional to routine intensified our defects. With one partic-
ularity: my defects were worse to her than hers were to
me. I was impatient and showed an unhealthy tendency
to suffer needlessly, at inopportune moments. Attenuat-
ing circumstances from my childhood might have

justified this to a panel of psychoanalysts, but in practice, my affliction was easy to confuse with a hardly dramatic but still tiresome jealousy. And besides that, I was getting boring. We don't talk so much about boredom, but I'd like to take the opportunity to state, here, in this conference for divorcees, that it is certainly the first factor to poison a relationship. I myself am so boring that, in my writing, I've had to elaborate a thoroughgoing philosophy of the grandeur of the dull, normal man standing up to the literary cliché of the insatiable adventurer and the embrace of movement, novelty, and fantasy. This is a stratagem meant to obscure the ease with which, even when I don't mean to, I slip into the insipid, tragicomic mode. It's true I've always known this, and it was easy to see it would turn into a problem at some point. But, without my really knowing why or how, our love continued, at least in appearance. And since we, the boring, are not bored by our boredom, I didn't see how much my boringness would eat away at the expectations of a person like her, a person who, by definition, wasn't boring—or was boring in a different way. And just because I did know boredom's each and every secret, I took it for granted I could usher us past that stagnation phase every couple has to live through, and moreover, that my failure to modify my habits made me the ideal person to do so. I've never been to a marriage counselor, but from what I understand, they generally recommend more communication, sincerity, conversations

about *us*. I, however, am suspicious of the elevation of
sincerity to a dogma. I have more regard for intuition
than for certainty. Since we both felt respected and the
affection was there and I had gone on greedily milking
the lottery factor, things were calm. By then I knew we
didn't make a good couple and that the discrepancy was
more my fault than hers. It's a simple question of mathe-
matics. If you take two people, and one has everything
you need to make a good mate for ninety-nine percent of
humanity, but the other doesn't, there's no need to look
any further. But I won't bore you with lurid asymmetries;
instead I'll get to the point. One day, on a trip to Portu-
gal, we visited the Santuário do Bom Jesus. You can get
there by car, but once you're in the parking lot, you have
to climb an endless set of stairs intended for pilgrims. I
remember the ascent as one of our great moments of
truth. Couples come together more through silence than
through words. On the way up, I started calculating how
much fatter I'd gotten since we'd met. It was an inopportune thought, but my skimpy résumé as a pilgrim didn't
present me with any better object of contemplation, and
my spirituality was precarious, just like my physical dexterity. Every flight of stairs gave way to another until, I
still don't know how, we arrived at last to the top. The
landscape was imposing, the sanctuary monumental, but
the effort had left its marks on us. If we'd existed in color
when we set forth, by the time we finished, we were

black-and-white. And then, emerging from a fissure in time, there appeared one of those itinerant photographers like the ones you used to find on the Rambla the century before. He had an old-timey camera, meant to impress unsuspecting tourists. It worked on us. He showed us a deliberately kitschy selection of photos. A frame shaped like a heart and, imprisoned inside, couples committed to happiness whose anachronistically naive expressions were fit for the girl and the soldier from the song "Baixant de la Font del Gat." But we were modern people, disdainful of our own feelings. And when we posed for that photo, we acted not with romantic sincerity, but with irony, more intent on the pleasure of parody than on the memory of an emotion worthy of framing. We struck a mawkish, hackneyed pose, but when the photographer gave us the picture a few minutes later—in black-and-white, like those melodramatic photonovels from the 1960s—I realized, thanks most of all to her expression and the gulf between her beauty and my pudginess, all of it made worse by the sacred stairway, that not making a good couple was no longer a coincidence. Quite the opposite; it was the heart of the question. But instead of admitting the truth—made plain by the ingenuity of the photographer, who chose, perhaps to spur on destiny, the image of us looking most defenseless—instead of being brave enough to suggest we end it then and there, without anesthesia, I chose to wait for the decline into boredom. And then and there, with the unequivocal diagnosis of the photograph in my hands, unable to celebrate the years of plenty, when love is borne forward by enthusiasm and shared affinities, I was neither generous nor wise enough to quit before I was fired.

MOTHER–SON
CHRISTMAS CAROL

.1.

My mother liked to repeat that the advantage of being a writer was that everything that happened to you could be turned into literature, sooner or later. It wasn't an original thought, and she tended to repeat it to encourage me to write when I was going through hard times. I remember that observation of hers used to drive me mad, but when she died and I was forced to adopt a more clement view of things, I began to grasp the rationale for this particular method of getting by. She'd lived through more disasters than all her children combined, and in literature as she practiced it, she found a therapy capable of recycling her dramas as narrative events suitable for sharing with readers. To test the worth of

her advice, I first had to convince myself I could write.
More from inertia than from ambition, I sensed that
I had the ability to shift from my own experiences to
those of others and back. I never had to be told imagination is a labyrinth that breeds introspective habits,
like sitting at the table day after day and filling endless
sheets of paper, observing and listening voraciously,
walking through the world with a head filled with
obsessions, ideas, fantasies. Or that if you stand firm
in this exercise—with a perseverance more often vice
than virtue—you will come to domesticate its mecha-
nisms, despite the torment of never conquering them
entirely, and you will cling to curiosity as to a compass.
This curiosity, instead of bringing me closer to real
life, draws me elsewhere, and so I toy with the codes of
fiction, more indulgent than those of reality. I say all
this as I write, knowing I will have to relate it sooner or
later to a thing that happened to me months back, and
another thing now on the verge of taking place. The
first was when my daughter told me of her first great
romantic disappointment, and I heard myself say to her:
"All these things that hurt so bad now, that you feel you
just can't take, will help you someday in the future." I
listened to her attentively, as always—even more since
we've lived apart—and I'm certain what she told me
saddened me. And yet my reply was just like the ones
that had incensed me when my mother used to utter

them, and I felt immediately ashamed. The second situation pertains to the doorbell, which will ring here in four, three, two seconds, one. In the world of fiction, a ringing doorbell on Christmas Day is typically synonymous with disaster or a sudden twist in the plot. But I happen to know it will be neither of these and interrupt my writing to open the door with a blend of expectation and concern. Right away, I recognize the woman who takes care of my neighbor in the upstairs apartment. Hastily, she tells me Ms. Encarna has slipped and fallen, that she can't pick her up on her own, and she asks could I please help her. Done and done. We climb the stairs, and the two of us get the lady to her feet. We sit her in a wheelchair while the woman who called at the door—I am too timid to ask her name—tells me she slipped and fell because there's too much wax on the parquet. As always when I enter another's home, I look at everything greedily: the mossy ground in the Nativity scene, the framed photographs, the painting of a soon-to-founder ship in the midst of a storm. This lasts no longer than three minutes, during which the woman informs me that she went to alert Paco but couldn't find him (Paco is the neighbor from the second floor, who, unlike me, does know his neighbors' names) and apologizes for bothering me on such a special day. Maybe because I'm in a period of undue vulnerability—I haven't gotten used to my new medication—I'm hurt that I wasn't the first

option; no disrespect to Paco. Fortunately, my thoughts
correct themselves no sooner than they've arisen, and
I realize that, even if Ms. Encarna lives on the fourth
floor, I on the third, and Paco on the second—which
means logically, she should have come to me first—still,
she's lived in the same stairway as Paco far longer, because I moved in only recently. All this occurs to me as
I confirm the indisputable excess of wax on the parquet
with a discreet but constant circular movement of the
sole of my shoe and ask Ms. Encarna if she's all right
and not what I really want to ask, which is: Why is she
spending Christmas without her family? And I am surprised when I notice Ms. Encarna looks a lot like my
mother, especially in the last memories I retain of her,
daunted by the awareness of her own disability. I realize
this similarity must have something to do with the fact
that all nonagenarian women in wheelchairs look alike.
But since we writers like to transform reality at our
whim, I permit myself the privilege of looking at Ms.
Encarna with the respect of a son for a mother before
saying goodbye to the woman whose name I was too
ill-mannered to ask but whom I wish a merry Christmas
all the same. Back at home, I try to remember what I
was doing before the neighbor rang, but I can't, because
a sense of urgency overtakes me. Urgency to write, with
no other purpose than remembering how my mother
used to always say that the advantage of being a writer

Mother–Son Christmas Carol

was that everything that happened to you—lovesick-
ness, a shipwreck, a newborn child—could be turned
into literature, sooner or later.

. 2 .

The proof of my mother's fidelity to her principles is that
once she could no longer recycle all that she'd lived
through in articles, books, and radio broadcasts, she died.
It seems brusque to say it this way, but the truth is that
she reached the outer edge of stubbornness in this technique for avoiding decrepitude. She drew on a philosophy
embodied in the more than thirty books she had published, all with a single theme—her own life—and thanks
to it, she didn't stop writing, not in the home she insisted
we send her off to because she didn't want to burden
anyone, not in her final two years, at the home of my
brother and sister-in-law, where she learned it's often
better to be a burden at home than a problem elsewhere. I
followed their evolution from caretakers to slaves in
detail, as their proud defense of my mother's independence (particularly after my father's death) turned to an
abject obsession with her every affliction. In the family
hierarchy, my profession as a writer made me the ideal
candidate to interpret—or try to interpret—her desires. If
I'm in the least bit honest, I would date the start of my

mother's deterioration from the moment she stopped using the typewriter. She lost the dexterity needed to type with her proverbial energy. With the pride of the self-taught typist, her skills honed in endless sermons denouncing technology as an instrument of capitalist alienation, she refused to make the change to computers. But, to prove she wasn't reactionary (*reactionary* was one of her favorite adjectives), she transitioned from a mechanical to an electric typewriter, and she considered this the pinnacle of progress. Her working method was inflexible. She wrote first by hand, in a script that, when I showed it to a graphologist, provoked several seconds of uncomfortable stupefaction, then typed out her drafts on carbon paper. When an article was published, she cut it out and archived it in one of her folders, which I will someday have to organize. She couldn't use the typewriter at the home, because a minor stroke had hindered her movements and her concentration. I offered my help so she could keep writing her weekly column for the newspaper. To avoid distorting this episode, I will transcribe what she herself wrote about it: "How do we manage to write and send our work to the editors each week without fail? First I compose the article by hand in a student's notebook, then I call my son, who shows up with his portable computer at the residence, I dictate the article to him, and he adjusts as he writes, making sure it fits the assigned number of characters. Once we're done, he saves this enormous file and goes home, where he sends it via email and verifies that it's reached its destination. The article appears on the page as planned, mission accomplished." We worked this way until her strength started failing, and she decided to say goodbye to her readers with one last column. But once we were no longer collaborating, she lost an essential reference point. She no longer read the papers with the eagerness of a person searching for a pretext to take part in public debate. We all encouraged her not to give in, we brought her new books—particularly poetry, which didn't demand such sustained reading effort—and I tried to convince her to record a kind of diary on a Dictaphone (I still have two, both unused). This didn't take a great leap of imagination: she'd already been observing the other residents for days, meaning to write a book entitled *Ninety Years Are Too Many*. I offered to pass her clean versions of the texts she scribbled out in a notebook and make any corrections she requested. It was a trying collaboration that allowed me to follow her decline in real time. She babbled and talked in circles, and this only confirmed how important it was for her to devote herself to her calling, even if only for a few hours. At the same time, the routines at the home, conceived to ease the employees' work more than to comfort the residents, made her life complicated. The vagaries of her health put an end to normality and led to rebellious tantrums that her medication made worse.

Sometimes my siblings and I had to put out fires without knowing whether she had started them herself, or even if they were actually burning. But sometimes our presence alone sufficed to soothe an outburst of paranoia occasioned by a supposed insult, or an *injustice*, if she was having an especially sanctimonious and revolutionary day. Things came to a head with the incident of the nail scissors she used, with a grotesque feel for the dramatic, to try to slice open her veins. You didn't have to be Freud to see it was an act of desperation, a cry for attention, and the resulting wound was negligible. But the protocols at the residence were as firm as my mother's will to breach them. Despite the trifling nature of what had happened, those in charge ordered a preventive consultation at the psychiatric hospital. In a dreadful mood, my mother burst into the consulting room for an interview with a young resident doctor, a circumspect Chilean who knew nothing of my mother's militant past or her status as an author. This ignorance might work in our favor, my brother and I wagered. Mistake. After the interview, the doctor (paler, with deeper bags under his eyes, and a bit less Chilean than he'd been before speaking with her) called us into an office worthy of the Albanian intelligence services. With an oncologist's gravity, he expressed his utter shock at the tale my mother had told him. "It's far from normal for a person to go on like that about the Civil War and her exile in Prague," he said, diagnosing these as potential symptoms of a novel form of delusional dementia. Had we not been so frightened, my brother and I would have shared a smile of melancholy comprehension. In a more deliberate tone than the doctor's own, we told him we would accept all responsibility—in writing, if necessary—but that, since the diagnosis was inconclusive, we refused to grant him authorization for the suggested days under observation or for experimental treatments of any kind. Unfortunately, comparable scenes of cartoonish insubordination piled up until my sister-in-law and brother, who live in Granada, offered to take my mother in and put an end to the dictatorship of *I don't want to be a burden.* We hatched a plan, a kind of neorealist kidnapping, with myself as intellectual coauthor and executive producer. The idea of a change of scene would attract her until it didn't. And since her mood swings were capricious, we had to view them as an obligation: getting her out of the residence as soon as possible. Brief mission report: I was in charge of hiring a large enough taxi to fit her in the back with the wheelchair and of mentally preparing the taxi driver (a dead ringer for Alberto Sordi) to show a Scandinavian sangfroid in case there was a flare-up of hysteria. My brother managed to remain heroically serene in the moments when panic was on the verge of paralyzing us and sabotaging our commando operation. The effort was worth it. My mother adapted wonderfully to her new surroundings, and the improvement in her mood was spectacular. In a few weeks, my brother contrived to convince her that, if she wanted, she could write again. He was bold enough to overlook her limited mobility and deposit a half-dead Toshiba laptop on the dining room table, and, despite all predictions and her anti-computer harangues, she learned to use it while continuing to scrawl in her customary notebooks. These were the last months she would exercise her vocation. She wrote with pleasantly reactionary tenacity. Often she repeated the same bit of text or variations on the same idea in the piles of documents that soon filled the Toshiba's entire desktop. In despair at their accumulation, my brother sent them to me via email. I edited them from a distance, relieved to no longer have to deal with the bureaucracy of geriatric residences or psychiatrists' Hippocratic circumspection. As if they were abstruse codices recovered from an archaeological dig, I deciphered these texts and, once they were corrected, sent them back for her approval or suggested changes. I felt analogically useful amid this digital back-and-forth. I understood then—as I understand now—the importance of writing, especially when you seem to have nothing else. When all she was capable of was the realization she could no longer go on, my mother threw in the towel. In those weeks, we all struggled to indulge her even more than usual. I rushed to prepare the (bound) anthology of her writings from the nursing home and Granada, brought them to her, and got her approval. With the same self-regard as when she was healthy and independent, she pronounced the book "very interesting" and asked me to talk to her editor about publishing it. It was a hard time for the editor. The publishing house had been robbed, and after a paranormal concatenation of misfortunes, a closure was in the works. Still, she found the time and energy to read the manuscript. Despite herself, she confessed that the text failed to do justice to my mother's reputation and that, for reasons of consistency and respect, publishing it would be counterproductive. We didn't tell my mother. We led her to believe the editor hadn't yet had time to look at it, and in doing so, we saved her a disappointment that would have done her in. Did we deceive her? Yes. But it relieves me to think that, if the situation were reversed, she would have done the exact same thing, treating us the same way parents treat their children around Christmas.

PATERNITY

Since age fifty, Omar has stood on the merry-go-round
of preventive medical exams. The verb that imposes
itself like a dogma on his increasingly infringed-upon
health is: *rule out*. From analysis to analysis and test to
test, the regular performance checks—as if he were a
vehicle—multiply his renunciations and the accompanying promises of improved quality of life in exchange for
the suppression of the assorted habits that had made him
very happy up to then. With resignation disguised as
curiosity, Omar, who has never been one to rush, adapts
to this new stage out of obligation to his family and his
work. At fifty-six, he's made it through numerous inspec-
tions until, at the most recent appraisal, after a sonogram
found nodules of uncertain provenance, the doctor ordered a urine analysis—not a sample, as is routine, but all

the urine evacuated over the course of a day. *To rule things out*, she said to him without a hint of irony.

After buying a special receptacle (more than two liters) at a pharmacy, Omar wonders whether he should stay home and, if he does go out, whether he should bring along the receptacle in a backpack. For scheduling reasons, he prefers to wait till Sunday to collect the liquid, to avoid complications related less to the procedure itself than to the niceties of its execution. At midmorning, he does what he generally does at midmorning: he goes to a matinee (a horror film, English, with characters made of modeling clay), and when he feels the urge to pee halfway through the film, he takes the receptacle to the restroom and back to his seat when he's done. No one suspects what lies hidden in the backpack, and when he leaves the cinema, Omar is happier with his uninterrupted routine than he is with the film itself.

After a frugal meal (at home, drinking the water prescribed to stimulate renal activation), Omar has a date with Amira, his daughter, to take the car out for driving practice. He has paid for her driving school to help her get her license; she's taken more than forty classes, but the results are far from encouraging. She's still nervous and still can't concentrate as much as she ought to on the relevant details of automotion. The proof is, the day they took the family car out for a spin to celebrate her passing her exam, she nearly ran over a pedestrian, a bicyclist, and a nun and blew through a red light and a crosswalk. To build her confidence, Omar has offered to practice with her until she achieves a level the two of them consider reasonable.

When they meet, Omar again feels an emotion that has evolved since they've lived apart. His sense of paternity had been figurative before, linked to details and tangible memories of Amira's life, as if the sum of the moments they'd been through formed the basis of a growing affection describable in rational terms. This accumulation of lived sequences contained difficulties overcome and assorted scenes selected by memory with chronological arbitrariness (an attack of gastroenteritis, a part in a play, volleyball games with Amira swinging from euphoric self-confidence to vertiginous depression, or a first love with turmoil and a morning-after pill). Since the divorce, Omar has noticed this feeling turning more abstract. It's no longer about details, situations, or an ensemble of experiences, but an emotional mass he can experience without needing to understand—and even if he wanted to, he couldn't—each and every one of its ingredients. It's as if each were confronted with the other's ignorance, as if they were speaking different languages but still held on to a biological bond on the outer margins of Amira's reality, where she was oblivious to her father's opinion or his capacity to intervene. Omar knows he can't be as stern as he'd like. That he has to

stifle his impatience and the sinister ideas that pass
through his head, that he must hide his perplexity when
such costly tuition produces a student so ill prepared.
"She won't take the test till she's ready," the head of the
driving school told Omar the day he signed up for ten
additional lessons. Now, though, in the passenger's seat,
he doesn't regret paying, and he smiles spontaneously
while withholding the comments that come into his
head while he watches Amira drive. What most surprises him is the lack of pattern her errors evince. In one
place, Amira demonstrates perfect knowledge of driving
rules and etiquette; a hundred meters farther on, she
forgets and breaks them with abandon. A few minutes
ago, for example, she was about to grind the gears on
the Carrer de Santaló, and just as Omar went to upbraid
her, she stopped serenely for a skater in headphones
who appeared out of nowhere, blissfully ignorant that,
if anyone else had been driving—Omar, for one—he
would already be dead. Amira made light of the ma-
neuver, her heroic reflexes, and the cosmic ingratitude
of the nitwit in question. And so Omar has praised her
insistently (when she was little, her teacher encouraged
them to reinforce her self-esteem, because Amira was,
by nature, easily discouraged), repeating in passing the
three basic concepts of driving: patience, prudence,
and anticipation. They've carried on without incident,
enjoying the smooth flow of traffic on a Sunday in the

springtime, not voicing the pleasure they feel at thinking of their own affairs. The gears change lithely; the
sound of the blinker marks each turn; there is a vague
sense of gratitude in the air, but then, at the roundabout
where Avinguda del Paral·lel meets Carrer de Lleida,
Omar notices the car is going too fast, and as they take
the curve, the backpack he left in the backseat tumbles
to the floor. He's annoyed he didn't foresee this, and
impatiently he orders Amira to stop the car. She does so
flawlessly: checking the rearview and the side mirrors,
turning on the emergency blinkers, parking, and pulling
the emergency brake. Omar has gotten out of the car to
see if the container's opened and notices with relief that
it hasn't. Curious, Amira asks what's going on, and he
tries to sidestep her before explaining, somewhat reti-
cently, the ins and outs of his unusual situation.

Amira is driving again, in silence this time, without
committing a single error. Just as she enters the parking lot and slides directly into her space, she asks Omar
about the thing he has already explained in part: "So all
day you have to collect your urine in a bottle you carry
in a backpack?" After he answers, she tells him goodbye
with a hug, more intense than the one she greeted him
with. Omar feels in it an unusual degree of certainty—
fatherhood offers such opportunities to access unwritten
codes—and he senses that Amira's opinion of him has
changed forever. What was once a sentiment determined

by conventions (priorities, signs, security protocols active and passive) is now entering a new stage neither Omar nor Amira is capable of imagining but that, he senses, will demand of them—of him, above all—a great deal of patience, prudence, and anticipation.

ON THE UTILITY
OF NOVELISTS

Let us situate ourselves in the arrivals zone at the airport and focus on the one person who is there neither for work nor to meet someone. He is a novelist, around sixty years of age, used to visiting the airport for the simple pleasure of contemplating a place with many people, constant changes of mood, and visual stimuli that nourish his fascination with the human race. Lacking any particularly unique traits, he passes unobserved on his way from parking to the elevator and advances, sure of his path, through the terminal. It's strange that he's smiling, because, in his public persona and in private, he has cultivated a taciturn grimace that tends to bashfulness or melancholy, depending on the circumstances. The airport lets him drop this mask and act naturally, and this sharpens his capacity for observation and refines his humor.

Just as there are those who never tire of staring at the sky, the sea, or fire, so he loves to watch the multitudes from a vantage point that takes in myriad details but also a comprehensive vision of the whole. He feels comfortable and secure in this panorama where vertices of space, light, and anonymity intersect. He could walk here with his eyes closed, but he prefers to keep them open, to confirm that the names of the cafés haven't changed since he was last here and that the most popular offerings are still the panini, the burger, the baguette, and the focaccia, brothers from one single polyglot, hypercaloric family. Like an inspector who can't help scrutinizing his surroundings, even on his off day, he approaches the salad and sandwich counters, the rows of industrial pastries, the beverages rich in sugars and artificial colors, notes that the flowerpots with their plastic plants are looking shabbier than ever, and tries to remember what the world was like before they invented rolling suitcases or mobile phones. But no memory has the magnetism of the present. And so he basks in it, aware that, unlike the majority of those bustling through the terminal, he hasn't come for any practical or professional reason or for tourism, but merely to enjoy the simple feeling of being here. Crack addicts say you only need one dose to get hooked, and that users are always trying to chase down the feeling of that first high. Fortunately, the addiction that has brought the novelist here is less tragic and more prosaic. His visits to the airport are sufficiently spaced out that, guided by his mood, he will inevitably hit on particulars that have eluded him before, as though general and episodic details were on constant rotation. Today, for example, he notices a certain similarity between the geometric choreography of the baggage carts and baby strollers and the people's hairstyles, which are arduously sculpted in a way he has never seen. And it surprises him to see that the chapel is empty, religious fanaticism and the superstitious un- certainty surrounding aeronautics notwithstanding. The novelist is thankful for the restraint of a group of people holding a placard to welcome back a well-known climber. Still, there are certain constants: the expressions of lovers carried away at the moment of reunion, or the contrast between those children who use their foreign surround- ings to act like monsters and those who fall victim to fits of narcolepsy hard to explain from a scientific point of view. The loudspeakers repeat: "Please watch your belongings." In one of the cafés, a waiter is wiping down trays while the automatic doors of the arrivals hall open and close like curtains on a vaudeville stage—and in front of them, gazes of curiosity, impatience, and exhaustion await embraces from mothers, girlfriends, sisters, grand- mothers, or grandchildren. An assortment of chauffeurs holds handwritten signs or tablets projecting the names of people they don't know. The novelist suspects the names are made up. He can hardly accept that a Nikolae

Tsiritotakis and a Matilde de la Motte inhabit the same world. To him—for an author, this is an occupational hazard—they carry a hint of espionage, of distortions of reality as evident as the intensity of certain perfumes or the imperturbable quality of faces so heavily caked with makeup they are incapable of articulating any concrete expression.

*And now, let's home in on the bar in the main café, specifi-*cally on a very tall woman who gets the novelist's attention with a gesture that denotes surprise and trust at once. It's possible you'll have the feeling you've seen her before. At the end of the twentieth century, she acted in a perfume commercial in which she steps off a high-performance motorcycle, removes her helmet, sniffs the assorted men at a party, lowers the zipper on her skintight leather body-suit, looks into the camera, and says, with exaggerated sensuality: "I'm not looking for just any man. I'm looking for Justin." This was the beginning of a long career of typecasting, with her voluptuous youth overshadowing her aptitudes as an actress. Years have passed, and the ad's impact has faded, but she still effortlessly draws the eyes of those around her. When the novelist sees he's being called to, his smile broadens; he approaches, re-marks on the years gone by since he last saw her, notices the passage of time has favored her far more than him.

Beauty is a gift, he thinks, and the actress has apparently borne hers impervious to the pressures of an age when an overly carnal interpretation of the roles she was offered subjected her to all the burdens magnetic sexiness entails. Proofs of this magnetism were not difficult to find. When he had first begun contributing to a daily newspaper in their city, the novelist hurriedly phoned her to propose writing an article on her, a profile, with the excuse of a show she'd been in that had garnered an enormous audience share. His reasons were as libidinous as they were harmless. But at their meeting, she impressed him as an intelligent woman with bright, shifting eyes who responded generously to each of his questions. Later, they would meet again in cultural spaces of one kind or another, but their chance conversations went no further than vague allusions to friends or interests in common. Their meeting today, he thinks, is one of those random occurrences done to death in movies and literature. The novelist uses the occasion to ask her what she's working on. It is then that he notices she's carrying a roll of cash register paper in one hand. It's not one of her usual accessories, and she tells him she needed paper to jot down a few notes and, since she had none, she asked for a bit from the waiter. Perhaps to impress her, he gave her a fresh roll from the machine as submissively as he would have done anything else she had asked of him. The novelist remembers that this power to impose her will through her beauty was what most fascinated him about the actress. Now he simply listens to her, and her words and the existence of the roll of paper unveil realities that again prove the wisdom of paying regular visits to the airport. She tells him she has chosen the bar over a table because from there, she can see the arrivals screen, and in the same tone, she informs him that her father has just died. That she is there to pick up her aunt, who's coming from Brussels. That the funeral is tomorrow and that, while she waits, she is making notes about what to say during the ceremony. At a loss, the novelist offers his condolences maladroitly and inquires into the circumstances of the man's death. The actress's answers lead him to think she hasn't yet fully absorbed the tragedy and is more affected by her logistical duties than by the impact of the loss. Then she says, when he least expects it, "It's good I found you here, you're a writer, you can help me with tomorrow's speech." She finishes by asking him various questions. Looking over her notes on the roll of paper, and, with a discipline they couldn't reproduce if they tried, she utters a series of thoughts, and the novelist restates them with more precise or less solemn alternatives, stressing the poignancy of some phrases relative to others. Now and then, the actress looks up, and, being tall, she can see the screen that tells her the flight from Brussels has yet to land. Such meetings often give rise to unease and discomfort between two people who don't know each other well and yet have no reason not to say hi. And so the novelist is surprised to find himself overstepping the bounds of discretion and throwing himself into the draft of the eulogy, with questions about the actress's relationship with her father. It's as if the strangeness of the occasion allows him to be different, more spontaneous, less judicious than usual. But just when he's started feeling comfortable with this unaccustomed brio, she realizes they've spoken only about her those past few minutes and asks him what he's doing at the airport. The novelist hesitates. The moment seems to demand he tell her the truth: that now and then he likes to up and go to the airport with no concrete purpose in mind, just to watch the people returning home and see how they greet the others after their absence. But he doesn't feel he should reveal so much of himself just now, and, since he doesn't know her well enough to say whether she'll understand or think it's the pastime of a snob or a psychopath, he prefers to take shelter in the practical conformism of falsehood: "I'm here to get my son," he says, "who's on his way back from Galicia." And when he starts to realize he's inventing too many details about this son he doesn't have, he stops and ends his reply with a smile less spontaneous than when he ran into her unexpectedly at the café. The novelist sees something neurasthenic in the actress's desire to finish her speech, as if her emotional control were only apparent and speaking at the funeral terrified her. He's too

well-mannered to dare to tell her that she's an actress, so
it will certainly turn out well, and it pleases him when,
after another glance at the screen, she tells him the flight
from Brussels has just landed and walks toward the doors
that open intermittently to reveal the endless spectacle of
newly arrived passengers on their way out. The aunt
emerges. She looks nothing like what the novelist has
imagined: a replica of the actress, but older. She is short,
in a straw hat, with abnormally red cheeks, and after hug-
ging the actress, she smiles with a joy that puts one in
mind of a pending vacation rather than the burial of one's
brother. The novelist attributes her restraint to the fact
that the family is Belgian. He even dares to say as much
to the actress, who, perhaps to pay her own respects to
the practical conformism of falsehood, replies that yes, it
could be; however much she loved him, her father was a
bit special, when you got down to it. At this point, the
author is happy. The visit has offered him more inspira-
tion than he could have predicted when he left home for
the airport. And so he goes on smiling and says an amia-
ble goodbye to the actress (and her aunt) just as the
climber emerges, preceded by a chorus of whistling, hur-
rahs, and applause. "Who's that?" the woman asks him,
seeing the welcoming committee unfurl their banner.
The novelist tells her, surprised at her ignorance of this
universally acclaimed athlete. And then, with a glance no
less fleeting than spontaneous, the climber catches sight

On the Utility of Novelists

of her, before he's had time to embrace the friends and family there to receive him. And if we focus on the mountaineer's expression, looking past the patina of jet lag, we can tell that he's recognized her. And that, with a blend of admiration and surprise, as if discovering an unknown virgin summit, he has drawn a line from her to the period, perhaps twenty years ago, when he was a teenager, paralyzed, just as he is now, at that instant when she appeared on television, got down from her motorcycle, took off her helmet, threw her hair back sensually, sniffed at her presumptive suitors, lowered the zipper of her leather bodysuit, and said she was looking for a man different from the others, and the boy—still unable to imagine he would one day become one of the most admired climbers in the world—wanted only one thing: to be Justin.

I'M NO ONE
TO BE GIVING YOU ADVICE

1. In the most tumultuous period of my adolescence,
   I used to fantasize I might be the son of Jorge Semprún. It wasn't an outlandish hypothesis. My mother
   and Semprún had been militants in exile, and despite
   the distance circumstances had forced on them, they
   shared a mutual respect embodied in the books of his
   lining the shelves of our home and his intermittent
   appearances in our conversations after meals. My father's role in expelling Semprún from the Communist
   Party during a fratricidal conference in Czechoslovakia
   only added a lurid attraction to the story. Impatient
   to hurry through all the requisite phases of childhood
   rebellion, I never wanted to kill my father, but I did
   want to hurt him. Semprún was among the pretexts
   my mother resorted to when she wished to question

the hierarchy—more political than familial—that my father incarnated. It was not always just an innocent game. Though reduced to the domestic environment, their dueling discussions included references to deep friendships bitterly lost due to politics and the accusation that the refusal to accommodate dissidence had destroyed what was best in the cause my parents believed in, even if their reasons for doing so were nearly antagonistic. In our home dwelled, on the one hand, a plucky communist, a defender of plurality (with a tendency to judge others according to her outsized sense of her own integrity), and the other, an official from the *Nomenklatura* marked by his obedience to party discipline (and the contradictions rooted in the successive metastases of the Soviet system). This gave rise to permanent, almost always fruitful debates; but on bad days, it could be a burden.

2. Perhaps it was nostalgia for youth, perhaps to get a break from the infallibility of the Central Committees, but my mother followed Semprún's activities closely, as a simple ex-comrade or member of that group of politically committed artists that included Yves Montand and Costa-Gavras, among others. My mother celebrated the success of Semprún's books, which were uncompromising in their condemnations of the Nazis but no less scathing with their critiques

of Stalinism. And when she noticed I was developing an unhealthy devotion to reading and writing fatalistic bombast in verse, she didn't hesitate to recommend them to me, as an antidote to existentialist posturing or else a sign of loyalty to a friend from her past. Likewise, when *La guerre est finie* made its debut, the presence of Semprún's name in the credits made him an obligatory reference in our talks about film. Semprún and his friends were successful, but beyond any other consideration, they were handsome. My mother repeated this with homespun frankness, celebrating a friend who had made his way into the glossies and the world of high literature, and her judgments on his attractiveness were harmlessly frank. In matters of men, she was more a connoisseur than an eclectic. She liked Humphrey Bogart, Jean Gabin, Robert Taylor, Albert Camus, Montgomery Clift, Lino Ventura, Yves Montand, Jorge Semprún, Sami Frey, Alain Delon, George Sanders, and, above all, Gérard Philipe. It took me half a lifetime to realize the only common denominator among them was their confidence in donning a trench coat with unmistakable elegance. This virtue could perhaps be ascribed to my father, who wore his trench coat with a distinction more of the correct and monarchical British school than of the Parisian, which was bohemian and anarchic.

3. Soon my adolescence, like a dealer lurking at the gates
of school to offer the students their first joint gratis,
gave me the opportunity to blaspheme the image my
father had cultivated. I must have been sixteen at the
time. The Unified Catalan Socialist Party and the
Communist Party of Spain were legalized. A way
of life in constant jeopardy up to then, one we had
talked about for many—too many—years, had finally
been normalized. The first few weeks were nonstop
euphoria and emotion. Everything had the allure of
the first time. The first night in a legal residence.
The first time my parents went to the cinema, to the
theater, to dinner without having to hide. The first
non-falsified ID. The first mailbox with first and
surname proudly on display. This process, though,
injected administrative disagreements into their customary political debates. My mother found, to her
disappointment, that our new situation did little to
change the habits of a man accustomed to delegating
everything to her, one who, with instinctive reticence,
failed to reinterpret his role as head of household
and to submit it to the laws of our new routine. On
account of his post now rather than the imperatives
of exile and stealth, he kept putting the party cause
before the duties the matriarch had imposed in our
new dwelling. The desacralization of my father was as
rapid as it was inevitable. And, eager to speed it on its

way, I used my devoted reading and Semprún's works to create a fantasy of alternative paternity.

4. If I had to speculate about the transition from the mythologization of my real father to the fictional rebel Semprún personified, I would have to look deep into my childhood. When I was little, our exile and life underground were governed by the logic of a greater good (the struggle against Franco), an automatic tribal loyalty (to communism and its liturgy), and heroes bound to an imperishable oral tradition. As long as Franco lasted, our priorities were clear. Everyone accepted their role with the conviction that things would change once normalcy returned. When the rule of law came, and the transition from pre-democratic Francoism to post-Francoist democracy imploded, the truth disappointed my mother's perhaps unreal-istic expectations. Overcoming limitations and the advice and prejudices of others, she had made herself a recognized, independent writer. Her other children were adults now, and I was the last one still at home, an overgrown baby taking advantage of the absence of authority, whether my father's or my brothers' (they were on their own or else in the military), to live the double life of a bad student and a devotee of culture in any and all forms. My passion was closely linked to the political ferment of the era. If at fourteen I wrote

poems of filial devotion immune to embarrassment
(my own or anyone else's), at sixteen I had to distance
myself from my recent past and declare an end to
childhood, histrionically squandering my innocence.

5. If before I had assimilated the family ideology by
   osmosis (Obelix didn't choose the strength and the
   appetite that define him), I would now discover,
   thanks to contagion from new friends and new places,
   the charms of extreme left radicalism, the republican
   Catalanism of the decadent bourgeoisie, political
   Christianity in its Capuchin guise, or better yet,
   the psychedelic, countercultural ferment that would
   enliven Barcelona until the attempted coup on Feb-
   ruary 23, 1981. Seventeen is a good age to act like
   an idiot and unconditionally confirm all the clichés
   about adolescent rebellion. The outcome: I bombed
   my college entrance exams and became a convert to
   a secular church that allowed me to act flip and ar-
   rogant, free from the duties and rigors of clandestine
   militancy. I practiced a subsidized, garrulous sub-
   version and, with the grandiloquence of an assembly
   of daddy's boys, demanded from all the politicians
   on the left a bravery and revolutionary fervor greater
   than the circumstances—the long shadow cast by
   Civil Guards in tricorne hats, the armored brigades,
   the executions by firing squad and *garrote vil*—would

allow. Impatient to discover the essence of a promised normality we had never known, my mother and I became the quality control sector for my father's new life. With predatory zeal, we audited his every movement, never noticing the look of nostalgia for his days in hiding that often crossed his face, when he didn't have to give explanations or bear the godforsaken contrariness of his wife—now a reference point for the left—or of a son who, without shame or the least idea of how to proceed, had gone from groveling admiration to rebellion like a slap in the face.

6. Semprún's books arrived in the midst of this inertia, radiant with the prestige of survival in the Nazi concentration camps. Since I knew one imprecise version of the story of his expulsion during the Fifth Congress of the Spanish Communist Party, and I had heard (garbled) murmurings about my father's role in Santiago Carrillo and Dolores Ibárruri's purge of dissidents, I reproached my father for ignominiously taking the Stalinist line against his valiant comrades. But my father was a touch deaf—a souvenir from Franco's torturers—and had a prodigious capacity for selective hearing, and I would like to believe my harangues didn't affect him in the least. Even as I look back indulgently, it remains curious that with his many sacrifices, my father should have to live

alongside admirers as uncharitable as my mother and myself. Admirers always ready—each for our own reasons—to lord over him a moral superiority which, at least in my own case, was scandalously refuted by a) my torpid refusal to avail myself of the privilege of studying; b) the flimsiness of the arguments that composed my diatribes; and c) even if the statute of limitations has expired, I will never forgive myself for this—my stealing money from him, a man who gave the lion's share of his salary to the party and lived in conditions of austerity commensurate with his ideals.

7. In a matter of months, the aura around my father plummeted like a stock with too much supply and not enough demand. For reasons of familial hygiene, my mother felt it was important not to succumb to the cult of personality that, with all the turbulence around us, would make of my father a symbol of communism with a human face and a kind of mascot sanctified by hard-liners, sympathizers, and even adversaries. The best way she could help him, in her mind, was to impede his deification so he wouldn't lose his principles or his sense of direction. "Loving him doesn't mean saying amen to everything," she declared. Outside the house, my father walked on air. For a few months, he recovered lost time and luxuriated in the love—a bit too much, according

to my mother—that the euphoria of the Transition brought his way. And he did so with the conviction that he had earned it and didn't have to explain himself to anybody. But his new role of legitimate politician, caught up in electoral disputes and congressional backstabbing, imposed obligations my mother disdained and that made our post-meal discussions still more bitter. A moment came when what mattered most to my mother was my father showing up on time for lunch or taking a perfunctory (not necessarily authentic) interest in my studies, not whether he was drafting a law to support gay rights or dignified access to abortion or working on plans for a general strike. I suspect that my father and mother's accord included clauses he hadn't honored to the letter and that, without the excuse of the political context and in an environment of apparent normalcy, she now demanded compliance with retroactive impatience.

8. Spurred on by my hormones, I added fuel to the fire. If I were to diagnose myself, the verdict would be dire: adolescence and intellectual pretense make a horrible cocktail. Fortunately, my father soon got used to the heat and now and then managed to force the conversation back to the classical repertory of soccer—Alcántara, Sagi-Barba, Samitier, Zamora—or

the *jotas* of José Oto, which we listened to with an
anthropological sort of respect: *Thirty parts sincerity
/ twenty of indifference, if you please / fifty of nobility
/ and you've got yourself an Aragonese.* Those were the
finest moments, when we escaped the conflict zones,
the demands placed on him (an incompetent in the
role of conventional father because he had never acted
as such) and those placed on me (more used to living
with a myth on a pedestal than with a father on the
front lines). Unlike my mother, my father had no out-
standing commitments or clauses subject to review.
We simply discovered each other, avoiding edging too
close to the abyss of having to admit we preferred our
clandestine past to freedom in the present.

9. Because I looked nothing like my father, it was easier
   for me re-create myself in light of the hypothesis that I
   was the son of Jorge Semprún. I did this unconsciously,
   enjoying the morbid charms of a sacrilegious fantasy
   far from improbable, at least on paper. The game was
   so absurd I never mentioned it to anyone. I suspect
   that it was structured in part by the antagonistic tensions inherent to adolescence: a longing for some sort
   of renown made worse by my parents' passage from
   covert anonymity to growing popularity—and the
   logical discomfort with everything my genetics had
   imposed on me.

10. This notion of an alternative paternity reached its extreme in 1977, when Semprún won the Planeta Prize for his novel *The Autobiography of Federico Sánchez.* The cover of the book showed a PCE badge identical to those we had around the house and, on the right, a black-and-white photo of Semprún in a trench coat. With his posture and his physiognomy, and the air of diffuse mystery the image exudes, it could have been a snapshot of my father in the darkest days of exile. Of my real father, I mean, who, in a hypothetical picture taken by Franco's police, would have revealed a similarly conspiratorial and dignified appearance. I have forgotten a lot about that time, I suspect because adolescence, unlike childhood, is something we try to erase quickly from memory. But I still possess my mother's copy of the book, with a dedication from the author. In the handwriting of a person used to admiration, Semprún has written: *To Teresa Pàmies, in memory of a (long ago) 5th Congress,* and, a bit farther down, the signature *JSemprún (Federico).* The *5th Congress* is the origin of it all, the lair of the Czechoslovakian disease that would consecrate the expulsion of militants who refuse to accept the directorate's partisan dogmatism. But the substance of the dedication, which lacks a date that would allow us to situate it in the continuous convulsions of that period, we find between the two sets of parentheses. The second

parenthetical, *Federico*, refers to Semprún's nom de guerre, recovered after so many years in this dedication (dashed off, I would like to think, in a cursory re-encounter with a friend standing in a line of readers, at once witness of the beginnings of all the book recounts and companion of one of the characters who appears in it as an antagonist). And the first, *long ago*, is coquettish, as though Semprún wished to underline his readiness to let lie a political drama of a kind common on the political left, which everyone, with self-induced amnesia, pretended to have gotten over.

11. Without reading the book, you might see this dedication as just the proper dose of courtesy. After doing so, it looks like a declaration halfway between cynicism and narcissism. And the surprising thing—and it strikes me that this detail was crucial to nourishing my fantasies of supplanted fatherhood—is that, even knowing of the contents of the book, my mother agreed to attend the presentation and waited—I know this to be true, she never made any effort to hide it—to greet her friend. In part because this must have been a way to reaffirm her idea that party discipline, taken to the extreme, had been a disaster, and in part to conform with her pugnacious militancy by reuniting, with an embrace at once urgent and chaste (in November 1977, when the book came out, my mother

was fifty-eight years old and Semprún fifty-three)
with an old friend now become the man of the hour
and the prototype of the leftist intellectual.

12. I devoured the book in a self-destructive fever. In it,
I sought confirmation for unfounded suspicions, jus-
tifications for fiercer criticisms of this father who had
reinserted himself in our everyday lives. It is a stark
and brilliant work about Spanish communist dissidence. At seventeen, I found it a respectful homage
to his comrades on the firing lines (whom I knew), a
virulent attack on the higher-ups (whom I also knew),
and a faithful portrait of the places that had marked
me, with a permanent army of comrades (Ramos,
Bernardo, Teresa, Julio, Gros, José, Tomasa, Román)
all clad in their respective trench coats. If childhood
is a time of fact interpreted through the lens of fancy,
adolescence is when we demystify the things we used
to glorify. And Semprún's book came down hard on
the facts but left demystification to the realm of opin-
ions (which everyone knows are veiled fantasies) and,
like the scripts of certain of his films, it was brave and
lucid enough to describe the communists as a tribe
condemned to loyalty to an impossible dream. The
most disturbing thing, more than anything else, was
the brutal, corrosive contempt with which he spoke
of my father. I'd be lying if I said it hurt me. To the

contrary: Semprún's rabid subjectivity supplied me with the perfect ammunition to go on metaphorically shooting my father down and to emphasize, from the pedestal of my own ignorance, the superiority of the right to dissidence over all other possibilities. And the increasingly tense conversations after meals (they were no longer a celebration or a prize, but an examination, a trial, an interrogation, and often a headache) encouraged me to pose as radical and principled and to watch my father take in my invectives with mute and generous indifference.

13. I wanted to knock him off-kilter and aggravate that gregarious Stalinism of his that Semprún denounces so feverishly in his book. But instead of reacting with rage, my father simply accepted, with the irony of an Aragonese (was that the twenty percent of disinterest or the fifty percent of nobility?), that his wife and son were committed, with policeman-like pertinacity, to talking to him about Semprún's book. Inured to the habit of imagining impossible situations to find answers to the questions no one would answer for me, I was inspired by my reading to consider the sacrilegious hypothesis of adultery. With absolute shamelessness, I dreamt up a brief meeting between Semprún and my mother that gainsaid the family legend that I was conceived the day my parents went

to see *Nights of Cabiria*, establishing a new origin, less Fellinian but just as cinematic. Now that I can no longer embarrass them, I write the following without any special enthusiasm: in my fantasized images of those clandestine Parisian encounters, Semprún and my mother (along with the theoretically cuckolded Aragonese) both wore trench coats.

14. Like the majority of adolescent deliria, this one too passed. It vanished from my mind as my father found a way to adapt to his new condition as a legitimate public figure. He didn't suffer the turmoil of a soldier returning from Vietnam or one of those political prisoners—Marcos Ana, Fabriciano Roger, Miguel Núñez—released after a sentence worthy of a Guinness World Record. Too old to give up the ideas he'd held on to all his life, too young to distance himself from his kinship to his clan, his sense of responsibility, loyalty, and discretion were such—as they had always been—that he withdrew from the front lines. Freedom from the omnipresent menace of repression and the codes governing life underground didn't modify his political goals, but it did change his habits. Working as an elected congressman three or four days a week in Madrid helped him recover the independence (and youth) he had partly lost and to enjoy an unaccustomed freedom. A freedom that would have

been subject to his family's quality control at home. Even today, I run into people who knew my father back when he regularly made the hop from Madrid to Barcelona and back. The memories they tell me in haste have little to do with politics but much with a nocturnal route of tangos, boleros, and *chotis* performed live amid laughter, flirtation, and more or less confessable discussions, free from the surveillance of party politics, with congressmen of all stripes taking part.

15. My alternative father, Semprún, would gradually lose that luster of perfection I had granted him in an error symmetrical to my prior idolization of my real father. I didn't like any of his books as much as *The Long Voyage* or *The Autobiography of Federico Sánchez*, but I read all of them with the discipline of a person doing penitence in secret. In not many years, I would have nothing left for him but the affection of an avowed reader and cinephile. Without intending to, I preserved a sort of mental attachment to Semprún that might extend to enthusiasm but would never again reach that fervent identification I felt in the flush of adolescence. I even followed his spell as minister of culture, when he managed to impose the prestige of the Parisian trench coat over the buckskin or corduroy of Spanish socialism. Yves Montand's character had

already foreseen all this in that scene in *La guerre est finie* where he says: *"Il y a des types qui sont clandestins et un beau jour ils deviennent ministres."*

16. In a film about those days, we would mark the passage of time with a sequence showing the pages torn away from a calendar or a sped-up procession of clouds, daybreaks, tides, and sunsets. And, to suggest the political realities, we'd add in archival footage of peaceful and violent demonstrations, silent marches of mournful multitudes against terrorism, and some athletic feat or other. In real life, though, my parents aged with slow dignity, as did Semprún. Apparently my mother saw him again at another conference and admitted—this time without political liabilities, and with the obstinacy of someone determined to maintain her rigor to the end—that she regretted both the docility capital-*H* History had imposed on them and her own minor episodes of meanness.

17. Once I had moved on through the tempest of adolescence to the more agreeable regions of early adulthood, I began to resemble my father. Chemically I mean, not physically—I would have been grateful for the latter—in a blood test that confirmed the same hypertension; and outside the laboratory, I inherited others of his manias, such as punctuality or the

inability to eat an egg without salt. The fictional son of Semprún withered away, only to rematerialize on exceptional occasions. Example: one day in Paris, I was talking to the editor Jacqueline Chambon, who told me she was a friend of Semprún's and that he had asked her with a measure of curiosity whether I was *my* parents' child. Jacqueline ended by telling me she was organizing a dinner at her home and would be inviting *the Sempráns*, in plural. The dinner happened, but at the last moment, the Sempráns dropped out. And though I had prepared for our meeting with clammy hands and a knot of expectation in my stomach, I felt relieved, perhaps because I knew by then that reality can never stand up to an admiration born in childhood and adolescence (with the exception of Johan Cruyff, of course; we are used to saying it's better not to meet our idols because they'll always disappoint us, but this never takes into account how much we must disappoint them).

18. Before I ever imagined I would one day write about my mother's predilection for men in trench coats, I bought one myself. It was at a flea market in Berlin in August 1987. I remember because the Nazi leader Rudolf Hess died a few hours before. The previous afternoon, I had stopped to rest in front of Spandau Prison, where Hess was serving a life sentence. I was

there on vacation, and I had rented a bicycle. On a
bike, cities seem more friendly and tourists less bar-
barous, and if there are parks, it's a pleasure to stop
in them and rest like a weary horse (even if here, the
motive for stopping was a raging irritation in my
inner thighs). What I remember from that trip was
the pleasure of solitude, the feeling of freedom, the
smoked salami from the hotel lunch, a cinema with
moth-eaten seats where I saw Andrei Tarkovsky's
Solaris in Russian subtitled in German, the bar Mi-
tropa, and the sensation of the rush of history at the
Olympic Stadium, at checkpoint Charlie, or alongside
Spandau Prison. I also remember that every night
after dinner, I would walk to Café Einstein, read
European newspapers in an introverted European
writer pose, and try to look interesting whenever
one of those women walked in who are used to men
trying to make themselves look interesting in whatever café they enter. I went there almost every night
for the three weeks I spent in Berlin, and despite my
struggles to impersonate the bohemian intellectuals
of Paris or Prague, I never managed to start even a
single conversation with a woman. But I did read the
headlines announcing Hess had died, and, spurred
on by the same temerity that had led me to fantasize
about being the son of Semprún, I mused that perhaps I'd had the paranormal ability to end the life of

the Nazi leader just by stopping a moment, the day
before, alongside Spandau Prison. Hess, one of the
men responsible for the countless tragedies Semprún
details in *The Long Voyage*, identical to those under-
gone by my uncle Joaquín and millions of other Euro-
peans with him.

19. It was dreadfully hot the day I applied my telepathic
powers to killing Rudolf Hess, and instead of wearing
my trench coat, I left it in my suitcase in the hotel.
I felt proud of the symbolic value of the purchase, a
secondhand trench coat from Berlin, of British man-
ufacture, and, idolater that I was, it recalled to me a
number of other trench coats I had admired in the
movies. Like the one Richard Burton wears in *The
Spy Who Came In from the Cold*, or Jean-Louis Trin-
tignant's in *The Conformist*. Or the one Boris Vian
wore everywhere with the desperate thrill of a man
who knew he would die young. Or the asymmetri-
cally comical ones of Jacques Tati. I wore that trench
coat for four years with an unhealthy perseverance
throughout the most nocturnal moment of my youth.
I was exquisitely shapeless, my anatomy best suited to
a poncho like the ones the singers from Inti-Illimani
wear or some similarly hopeless garment. The trench
coat was a symbol of inaccessible elegance. It was the
attire of choice for the actors and authors I admired,

and when, years later, I met Anna, I tried to impress
her by buying her a trench coat, red with a leather
collar, that cost me two months' salary (it goes without saying she never wore it, but she still owns it,
maybe as inculpatory evidence against our relationship or in the hope that one of our children will take a
liking to it and adopt it as part of their repertoire with
the same nostalgia we had shown, as a sign of our
unqualified modernity, by donning the clothing of
our own parents).

20. I read so much Semprún I wound up boring myself.
I didn't admit it, but I found him repetitious and a
wee bit of an exhibitionist on the subjects of survival
in the camps, life underground, and his unjust expulsion from the party. He reminded me of a comment
from my uncle Joaquín, who divided survivors of the
Nazi camps into those who wrote and lectured about
their experiences profusely because they hadn't spent
enough years inside and others, like him, who'd had
their fill of privation and horror and got out with
the sole ambition of forgetting, convinced that there
was no point in trying to describe them. But a bond
of respect remained, the understanding that writers
tend to obsessiveness by nature and that returning
to the scene of the crime was a sign of desperate
consistency, not of posing or a loss of powers. Régis

Debray, who knew Semprún well (and who wore trench coats of the Social Democrat cut), sees him as a privileged member of what he calls the *aristocratie du malheur*. And, with the conceptual maneuvering typical of brilliant intellectuals in decline, he affirms that Semprún "privatizes History at the same time as he *historicizes* his own life." What is most interesting, though, is when Debray, who would share with Semprún the same addictions and the same ideological detox cures, describes his friend as an old man who uses memory like a mirror to look what he once was in the face, and who finds there dozens of avatars, each insisting on a quota of heroism that will prevent them from becoming zombies; and we will never know if these personae are real or invented.

21. I distanced myself without bitterness from Semprún at the same time as I began, slowly but with perseverance, to recuperate my father. Not through politics but through continued practice of my role as son, without the interference of history now, beginning a normal relationship (assuming the adjective *normal* is ever applicable to father-son relationships). Becoming a father myself had granted me a perspective immune to ideological prejudices, and, instead of drawing on my surplus energy to kill or wound my parents, I tried to make myself useful and care for them, more

from responsibility than from conviction. I didn't
see it then, but my parents had left me an immate-
rial legacy in lieu of heritable property or monetary
instruments. They invested their entire lives in com-
munal ideals and had followed that decision rigor-
ously, but they gave my brothers and me the chance
to distance ourselves from politics in general and
communism in particular. At times, tempted by the
byways of creative supposition, I imagine my mother
was the one who opened the door for us and pointed
us toward a less turbulent way of life, and my father
accepted this with the same ironic complaisance with
which he accepted so much else. If they resigned
themselves to the imperfect democracy of asymmet-
rical consensus and reconciliation, we were allowed to
choose, without urgency or sacrifice, to perpetuate the
struggle via legalized militancy or be sucked into the
inertia of middle-class conventionality or the questioning of ideology as a whole. It wasn't until my own
children started to grow up that I looked around and
realized, for better or for worse, that they had gotten
through life without ever experiencing even one of the
ideological intrusions essential to my childhood and
adolescence.

22. In my father's closet there was a trench coat I didn't
care to inherit because, with my post-Berlin euphoria

behind me, I had renounced all presumptions of elegance (it was enough for me to go unnoticed in the universe of those who, in questions of attire, content themselves with myriad parkas, windbreakers, blazers, and anoraks). In the meantime, my father had begun to shrink and hunch over. He shed his girth and the air of authority it granted him and took refuge in the timid constancy of his coats. Memory is cruel, and witnessing my father grow old, accompanying him to his many medical exams, lending him a hand writing his memoirs (with the tireless assistance of Enric Cama), relegated Semprún to an increasingly minor role. He was an incidental presence, he no longer formed part of my family history, and I didn't really think of him except when he wrote an article about memory and intellectual commitment or when he was called on to commemorate, as he did once at the Palau de la Generalitat in the presence of my uncle Joaquín, the heroism of the survivors of the Nazi concentration camps with one of those brilliant speeches of his.

23. Let's turn again to the cinematic portrayal of passing time and add in a few scenes of rain, images of the patios of Parisian cafés, or cemeteries that inspire melancholy. Let's introduce scenes of political unrest, in Prague or in Berlin, to give the sense that the story

is moving forward amid those surging conflicts where leaders in trench coats inevitably appear to address the febrile masses. In the family, this acceleration of time, which arbitrarily elides long, seemingly dull stretches to focus on the events that mark the pulse of kinship, makes itself felt in funerals and visits to the hospital on account of illness, but also in the celebration of the newly born not forced to live with the same historical intensity as their ancestors.

24. Whoever believes the trench coat can express only revolutionary charisma or bohemian romanticism is wrong. Many images attest to its thorough transversality, its adaptability to the most admirable and committed sorts of humanism as well as to genocidal totalitarianism. To dissidence and stirring creativity, but also to abject and megalomaniacal violence. To put it plainly: Hitler and Stalin both wore trench coats, and so did the torturers in sinister sunglasses in Argentina and Chile. Does knowing this lessen my desire to write about the influence of the trench coat on my family history? No, but it forces me to be more of a journalist than a storyteller and to pay a visit to the family closets, which my mother kept pristine with an air of mystery and immense doses of naphthalene. The moment when we brought out the winter clothing was a highly anticipated ceremony, and I,

sole witness to my family's calmer period (without brothers at home, and with my father off sampling the pleasures of legality), was able to experience it firsthand. If he had put on weight, my father would remove some blazer or other from his wardrobe, and I would inherit it—I still have a few—with an enthusiasm not feigned in the least.

25. Then, many years later, the surprise. When my mother died, I found two hand-sewn trench coats in her closet. And I didn't recognize them, not because she'd never worn them, but because, unlike my father, who was always gone and hence remembered as a hero, my mother never enjoyed the privilege of being idolized by her children. She'd had to play the bad cop, quality control for husband and sons, and if her energy didn't suffice to please everyone, she always had enough to do—at a time when everything was harder, more uncertain, riskier—what was right. Finding those trench coats triggered the memory of times when my mother used to wear them without our noticing. She donned them with the satisfaction— her pride in her sewing could be compared only with her pride as a writer—of participating in the fashion of her time. A fashion that exploded as soon as Paris and Prague decided to institutionalize the trench coat as the informal uniform of chic dissidence.

26. It is time to think about bringing this tale to an end. My father has grown old following the precepts of José Oto's *jota*. He is a demanding but lovable invalid. During checkups, he has turned over to me the responsibility of talking with doctors and supervising treatments and dosages. Since he is a man of some renown, there are specialists who go out of their way to be kind to him. Though they've detected in him two simultaneous cancers, there is still one who tells him neither of them will kill him. As he transmits this information in an ominously patronizing tone, my father responds with what remains of his sense of humor: "Then I suppose we should be happy, right?" His deafness is isolating him and his character is clouding over, especially if we recall his professional and personal inclination to charm. In discussions after meals, my parents' old age, shared as tenaciously and affectionately as ever, has done nothing to uproot their differences, but if politics hasn't gone away, more earthly problems now have pride of place: questions of health and of a lifestyle composed of falls and physiotherapy, diets low in salt, and of course, the funerals of comrades and friends.

27. Space has now dwindled almost as much as time, and the closets are full of trench coats unsuited to the season, but then one day, meteorologists announce

a cold front coming, as God has willed that cold fronts should, from Siberia. My father is in a wheelchair now, and we go out every day for a walk. As he hunches over in his chair, his old trench coat hardly fits him. I tell my mother this, and she authorizes, even urges me to go to El Corte Inglés and buy what she calls, with uncharacteristic imprecision, "a nice parka." My father and I still don't look alike, but he has shrunk and I have swollen, and we now possess equivalent heft. And since it's hard for him to lift himself from his wheelchair, he asks me to try on the garments so he can choose the one he likes best. We navigate the *gentlemen's* floor, as we did when I was little and he would take me to look at Christmas gifts. With a practiced touch that recollects his faraway days as a tailor, he feels their texture and offers expert commentary now and then. He's in a good mood until he falls in love at first sight with a Burberry trench coat with plaid wool lining. The employee on the floor approaches, praises his selection—they always do—and watches my father try it on via an intermediary: myself. I hold out my arms like a scarecrow, stretch my neck upward, feel the flawless warmth of the wool, and regret our not owning an appropriate hanger for what must be far and away the costliest garment my father has ever bought. He observes me, sustaining the beginnings of a smile partly shadowed

by cancers the doctors say won't kill him. I don't
think about how, ten years after his death, I will write
this story that is possibly too diffuse, with too many
adjectives and adverbs. We take the coat, and unlike
many other political and domestic choices systemat-
ically criticized by my mother, this one is applauded
and accepted as an element that will define the
late-period attire of my father, who was set on wearing it even when the weather didn't justify it.

28. Let's speed things up, because I don't feel like linger-
ing on the agony in the hospital. Or on the funeral he
would have liked but didn't get because my mother
lacked the willpower to deal with all the protocols. Or
his absence, endured with little privacy because my
father had an unalterably public dimension. We will
leave time to impose its criteria and banish my father
to the oblivion of limbo which, in my family, is as
much an act of remembering as of forgetting. Let the
children get old, and the babies grow up. Watch as
they tattoo cryptic phrases on themselves, get pierc-
ings and dye their hair in Benettonic colors. Let us
insert scenes with arguments that lead to separations
or silence. Arrange it all in a political context where
someone tells us, now and again, what our parents
would have thought and done, were they alive. But
they are dead. And among all the things they've left

behind and the legacy we children administer as best
we can, there are distinctions, medals, requests for
tributes to be politely dodged and municipal deci-
sions about perhaps changing the name of some tiny,
tucked-away plaza, and reprints announced with
emotion eventually shattered through symptomatic
indifference.

29. But there is a more intimate dimension: my own
closet. I have just one, because I live in a small apartment my parents never came to visit. I keep clothes
there that are generally too small for me and that I
hold on to because, like all obese people, I think I
will one day be thin again and once more able to wear
them. I have two of my father's suits there, in case I
ever get married, die, or receive a prestigious prize,
plus a half-dozen ties I wouldn't know how to wear
(I never learned to tie the knot) and the trench coat
from El Corte Inglés, as sturdy as it was when we
bought it. And, on rare occasions, when the Siberian
cold decides to stop back in at Barcelona, I like to put
it on. Like today, after hearing the meteorologist on
the radio let a phrase slip that defines in moral terms
the moment we are living in. He said the temperature
would be low, and that late in the day, there would
be "faint groups of frail clouds." At first I thought
that was a good title for a book of poems, but the

impression quickly vanished. I've taken the trench coat out of the closet. It doesn't smell of naphthalene, because now there are odorless clothespins that—allegedly—ward off the moths just as well. I have to leave for a work interview—it is what it is—and I miss those few moments when, in similar situations, I would ask my father's advice. The last time, I spoke to him about an emotional crisis that wound up being definitive, but he was by then in a phase of incurable renunciation and told me he was no one to be giving me advice. I was surprised, because one of the few universally recognized tasks of fathers is giving their sons advice, and I assumed that, for the sake of biographical consistency, he preferred to remain an absent father to the end. But today I want to make a good impression, and I know the trench coat will help. At first, I'll feel a bit strange, as I always do when I put it on. But I also know the melancholy about to invade me will be not sad, but comforting. And when I pass by a display window, I will look at myself from the corner of my eye and reconfirm something I already know. That no matter how I try, I will never know how to wear a trench coat with the carefreeness and elegance of my father, Jorge Semprún, and all the men my mother liked.

PLEASE

They got here early in the morning: two girls and three boys, crammed into a rented Hyundai driven by my son. They unloaded the materials and, as we agreed by phone, have overtaken what we call *the yard* by common accord, though it's really just a plot of weeds used as a depot for moribund objects. My son looked rather taciturn, but this isn't a new impression: it has to do with the idealized memory I have of when he was little and laughed all the time. I've left donuts and coffee on the dining room table, in case they want breakfast, and have taken shelter in my study, too far off to be a bother but close enough to have a good view of them filming. My son hasn't introduced his friends, who limited themselves to greeting me from a distance and striking poses like the bleak cineastes they dream of being. Now and then, one comes over to ask for something without saying *please*: a lighter, an ax, Monopoly money, rope, a bit of gauze. I try to assist without making maladroit remarks. On one of these trips back and forth, I notice the sockets in the kitchen and dining room are all occupied, probably charging cell phones or camera batteries.

Since I've lived in this house, I've refined my ability to pretend I am working to a maximum degree of unproductivity. I spend hours, days, and nights stranded on the internet, catching waves that carry me away from the translation—an article on pediatric pulmonology—that I should have finished three weeks ago. The publisher hasn't asked for it, but the guiltier I feel for blowing my deadline, the less willing I am to work. With the windows open, I try to catch bits of the characters' dialogue in the short film. I must be losing my hearing, because all I can make out are the most obvious commands, *action* and *cut*, both uttered by my son. The rest of the words are an inaccessible whisper, spoken with deliberate vagueness, interrupted by a laughter more smug than joyous. Once in a while I get up, go over to the window, and look at them without bothering to hide. I try to situate the actors' movements within the two-scene script my son emailed me after asking over the phone whether he could use my house to film. Before hanging up, I remember, he said to me: "Oh, by the way: you'll be in it, you'll have to play dead." Just like that, without adding *please*.

After listening to my son's instructions, I try not to annoy him. Seeing him directing and giving orders and advice makes us both feel uncomfortable. That must be why he saved my appearance for the end, after a productive morning without setbacks. In these unusual situations, it unnerves us to have to reveal ourselves as we are to those closest to us. With this in mind, I have adopted the professional attitude of the duteous extra. When the director asks me to lie down on the ground, telling me the short's protagonist—a young man with a beard like an apostle—will grab me by the feet and drag me through the yard, my only question is how to hold my arms. The response is hardly convincing, but still, I don't argue: "Hold them like you're dead."

As I lie on my back on the ground, I feel a stabbing sensation near my right shoulder. When my son was little and he used to get sick, I would calm him down by asking if the aches and pains he felt were familiar or new. It was almost always a pain he recognized, and saying so helped him understand it wasn't so serious and made him more obedient when we told him to drink water or take medicine or a spoonful of broth or apple compote. The jabbing feeling I notice just now is like none I've ever experienced. Since I don't recognize it, I analyze it. It radiates with retractile motions, some to the right, some to the left, some up toward the surface, and some down in the direction of intestinal depths I didn't know existed. The cadence is repetitive and grows more intense, like Ravel's *Bolero*, and other instruments (esophagus, lungs, trachea, heart) seem to chime in, with the same melody, but increasingly alarming. I don't connect the pain with death, only with fear, and just when I want to tell the bearded actor dragging me along to let go of my feet and stop, I realize all my strength is gone and the most precise way to define my present state—precision being a professional vice of those of us who work with words—is *dead*.

Death, surprisingly, has the structure of an hourglass. While I slip off toward who knows where, I am far more conscious than when I was alive. It is as if I had the opportunity to take leave of myself not by watching my life in reverse, but instead in this final moment. The first thing this burst of lucidity tells me is I won't be able to finish the translation. The second thing I think of is the chargers: I wonder if they'll blow a fuse. The third, a bit ridiculous given the situation I'm in: the actor, following my son's instructions, has been dragging me around for quite some time. From what I understand, in this scene he is supposed to get rid of my body, but the actor must have realized something isn't right, and he's hesitated and finally stopped, leaned over, looking at me closely (beyond the part of his face covered up by his beard, a mix of panic and perplexity suffuses him), and shouted that I seem to be dead. And then I hear my son's voice, with a determination of uncertain origin (he certainly didn't get it from me), yelling at the sinister cameraman: "Whatever you do, don't stop filming!"

THE PHENOMENOLOGY
OF THE SPIRIT

*In car 2, seat 9C of the Madrid–Barcelona high-speed
line,* I cry. Concentrating on one of the screens, with
the headphones plugged in, I am watching a romantic
comedy about time travel. Again, it surprises me how
easily watching films gets me worked up and how monstrously inexpressive I am when the drama is real. The
landscape filing past in the windows seizes my attention
and fills me with the cadences of that sinuous horizon
advancing in the opposite direction. The long stretches of
parched land remind me of Republican poets and Fran-
coist painters. The hills of charred trees and the majesty
of the wind farms move me. Thrashed by the breeze,
the clouds scatter menacing shadows on the grain fields.
My tears, with the consistency of eye drops rather than
of grief, coat everything I see with an overly lustrous

varnish. Destiny has placed me next to a onetime Socialist minister of education. He's a discreet man, affably
ugly and unusually large. He's wearing a sky blue shirt,
glasses that reveal a disregard for fashion, and lace-up
shoes, probably made to measure (I'd reckon him for a
size 16.5). For some time, he's been reading a newspaper
I write for. When he reaches the page with my article
for today (a review of a TV movie about Bishop Pedro
Casaldàliga), he skips over it with an indifference that,
instead of offending me, brings a smile to my face. When
he's done, he orders a Diet Coke from the drink cart and
starts talking on the phone—a Samsung smartphone
with a leather case—in a voice so low it's impossible to
hear what he's saying, unlike the passenger in 10C, who
has shouted three times: "If we solve the connectivity
problem, that won't happen." With the movements of a
man accustomed to taking advantage of every minute, the
ex-minister removes from his bag a student's edition of
Hegel's Dialectics, a printed text—a lecture, I'd assume—
and other study materials he marks up with a red roller
ball (Pilot) in the margins or highlights with a fluorescent
marker (Staedtler). His handwriting is elegant but hard to
read. From the corner of my eye, I keep trying to decipher
it, but all I can make out are words like *the Greeks* and
masters underlined in the manner of experienced lecturers
who wish to emphasize an idea or mark the departure
point for those digressions that are often more interesting

than the essential substance of their presentations. When
the ex-minister yawns, I realize I'm no longer crying,
and I pick up where I left off in the film. Unlike the protagonist, I am able neither to travel in time nor to share
the message—we should enjoy the splendor of the insig-
nificant moments of our life—revealed in the comedy's
climax. A half hour before I reach Atocha Station, the
film ends with a song that stirs me up again. I'd like to
call someone and ask, do you love me, even just as a joke,
but, wisely, I resist the temptation. Unnerved, I grab the
notebook I always carry like nitroglycerin tablets prescribed by a cardiologist and try in vain to write something. To make myself interesting, I imitate the other
passengers' hyperactive gestures. I look at the screen of
my cell phone—an antediluvian Nokia—and confirm:
no messages and no missed calls. When the train stops,
I am one of the first to get out, and with an embarrassment I alleviate by rushing toward the exit, I pretend to
be talking on the phone. I answer in monosyllables, feign
laughter at an inside joke, and with a forceful, determined
voice, wishing to make myself heard, repeat, "If we solve
the connectivity problem, that won't happen."

BELARUS

The setting for this story is a dog pound. Your children are the protagonists, and you have a supporting role. Your daughter is the leader of the expedition: the first to enter the building and speak to the receptionist. She tells her the purpose of the visit: she wants to give her mother— Anna—a dog, but instead of going to a pet store and buying just any puppy, she'd rather seek out expert advice. You are surprised at how she expresses herself without hesitation, as if she'd acquired a self-assurance unthinkable just a few years before. Your son, on the other hand, on the far fringes of apathy, never looks up from his cell phone. The volunteer helping you gives *a quick rundown* of the conditions for adoption. She addresses you in particular, perhaps because you seem to be the one best placed to sign the form, which you don't hesitate to fill out. When you're done, she proposes you visit

the dogs while she recites a speech she seems to have
given many times about responsible ownership, the trial
period to see how the animal adapts to the family, and a
series of adoption requirements—complete vaccination,
deworming, neutering, ID chip—that sound like the fea-
tures of an electrical appliance. "When you find one you
like, tell me and you can take it out for a walk," she says.
She notes your surprise at the idea that an animal can be
tried out and adds that this will help you see if the animal
is defiant, hyperactive, or calm, and whether you have
chemistry with it. You remember a documentary about
adoption and the story of a worker in an orphanage in
Belarus who talked about the strategies the children—the
candidates—used to seduce potential parents. The children had only a few seconds to win them over with looks
that inspired compassion or shows of affection or obedience. Following the volunteer, you reach a series of hall-
ways with cages, looking more like a refuge than a prison.
In each is a dog, its name—*Pipo, Brown, Laika, Goku,
Lula, Roc*—written on the door in letters too childish to
have been written by a child. The animals' eyes show
their longing for love, for freedom and attention. The
volunteer tells you that taking them for a walk means
they can trade their isolation in a two-square-meter cage
for company and space in the garden. She says this in a
neutral tone, but you take it as a form of pressure, maybe
because this entire mission makes you uncomfortable.

Belarus

When your daughter stops in front of a cage, exchanges
glances with the lively beagle inside, and affirms that
Anna will definitely love this one, you don't know what to
say. Your son snaps photos on his cell phone. You've had
doubts about this from the beginning, but you felt it was
better to indulge your children's initiative than to repress
it, as usual. For months now, you've seen a deterioration
in the family's situation; all of you are lapsing into a
mechanized respect that camouflages the routines of
mutual isolation. You don't know how to relieve this feeling of distance. When you try, you sense Anna pulling
away from you exactly as far as you do when, with ever
less frequency, she tries to do the same. The mere fact of
exposing your reciprocal goodwill is hastening a rupture
you still believe you can somehow avoid. Your children
know this, too, but since there are no arguments, no
screaming and crying, it's easier for them to give in to
their tacit, not especially visceral resignation. The days
pass as the weeks do, without shrillness, without apparent
changes. Both you and Anna have a bomb maker's in-
stincts, and when you detect the risk of conflict, you take
the measures necessary to avoid an explosion. This is the
backdrop for the idea of buying her a dog. Your children
took the initiative. And since they so rarely show initiative, you decided you wouldn't overrule them. You agreed
to visit the dog pound (you now know its official name is
the Companion Animal Recovery Center) and to make a

decision "depending on what we see." The problem is that they've taken this as a yes, and, standing in front of the beagle with the glimmering eyes, proudly sporting a visitor's sticker on their chest, they've let the novelty of the idea get the better of them. Anna has never been a great lover of animals—nor have the children, not till recently. In their childhood they never had turtles or hamsters, not even a goldfish. But in the past few months, they've started talking about dogs, even if, for you, they really did so only for the sake of having something to talk about. It's true that in those conversations—alternating with the increasingly symptomatic clink of silverware on plates—Anna seemed unusually receptive. That, plus a number of cosmetic changes (cutting her hair short after decades wearing it long, or tattooing a yellow star on her ankle), convinced your daughter to decree that now it was time for a dog. To add weight to her conviction, she surprised you with the following declaration: "We"—meaning she and her brother—"won't be living with you forever." You don't care to rebut her by saying that most likely, you yourself would have to leave before the dog arrived, let alone before either of them reached adulthood. Still, you remember, you couldn't stop staring at the beagle. While it wagged its tail with the cadence of a metronome, it pointed its muzzle and ears in the direction of the garden. The children asked its name, and all of you smiled when the volunteer replied, "Buddha." That

Belarus

name, you realized, more than just the sight of him, was a factor in your connection to him. He wasn't fat, and he didn't give off that feeling of inner serenity attributed to Buddhists, but once you knew he was called Buddha, it was hard to imagine him with any other name. The novelty getting the better of them, your children wouldn't stop saying "Buddha!" as if they wanted to test out their aptitude for owning him. In the morning, before you left home, you lectured them about the importance of responsibility, but you ran into an unbreachable wall of ignorance and enthusiasm. "Mama will walk it," your son argued, "that's why we're giving it to her." On another occasion, you would have butted in and argued on this point, and you would have made them promise to take turns. But it strikes you that, as they grow up, you need to give them more space, so you don't demand this of either of them. Meanwhile, Buddha took advantage of his supervised freedom to run the way dogs do: aimlessly. He didn't bark once, and his restraint leads you to suspect that, like the Belorussian orphans, a dog that is a candidate for adoption must sense that barking makes a bad impression and is forbidden. Not barking, on the other hand, was advantageous, because when the potential adopters went home—and novelty got the better of them—the children, those truly in charge of the final choice, would almost certainly remark approvingly: "Did you see how he didn't bark once?" The volunteer lent you a leash so you could walk him for a few minutes, and you observed how Buddha scored goal after goal and none of you put up any resistance. You even stopped to reenact the universal gesture of throwing a stick and waiting for him to bring it back. And, with a prodigious show of obedience, Buddha knew to start running while the stick was still in flight, retrieving it and submissively approaching your daughter, as if conscious of which alliances served him best. To avoid giving in to the most obvious emotions, you forced yourself to imagine the scene with Anna there. The image that came into your head was of uninterrupted contrariness, as if, posed in front of the Christmas tree—absurdly artificial, because your children are now sworn adversaries of real firs grown on a farm—she would accept the gift of the dog in a way that made plain to everyone she hadn't actually liked it. Perhaps to rescue you from these spiraling ruminations, Buddha came over to sniff at your loafers. He didn't seem tired, and he raised his head to look you in the eyes with categorical candor. Your son wouldn't stop taking pictures and repeating, "I'm going to post them on Facebook." After a moment, you returned to the gallery of cages and the volunteer asked you how it went and noted your response with satisfaction, trying to gauge your degree of commitment. You asked, still doubtful, if you could put off the decision until tomorrow. "No problem," she said, but your children looked surprised, and you had to explain that you just wanted to sort out the details. You didn't say as much, but they took this to mean the adoption was a done deal, and you brought the documents and flyers with you as if they were a signed contract. In the car, the conversation continued. Your daughter resolved all the open questions: Where would he sleep? Who would walk him? Was there a vet close to home? What you thought were objections she enthusiastically parried, bringing them back the original purpose of the gift and the certainty—which in reality was only a hypothesis—that Anna would love him. Finally you turned to the question of delivery. Christmas was coming soon, so you'd have to act fast. You would pick him up tomorrow once the formalities were taken care of, and you gave up the idea of wrapping him in a big box only because your son emerged from his lethargy to ask you, "What if he's claustrophobic?" As you made your way home, threading the exits on the Ronda de Dalt like the beads on a rosary, you each fell back into your customary isolation. Glued to their phones, your children laughed, raised their eyebrows, and furrowed their foreheads to messages you can only imagine, focused as you are on your driving. It hit you that you'd like to prolong that intimacy they'd shared with the dog not long ago. Or talk again about your goal of a Christmas not doomed to inertia, to giving each other handkerchiefs and scarves destined for the drawer for handkerchiefs and scarves you never wear. To distract

yourself, you wondered why so many gifts wind up aban-
doned, but slowly, you couldn't help but notice a more
prosaic uncertainty taking hold. The uncertainty of
whether this gift was a good idea. The fear that, if not on
the first day, then after a couple of weeks had passed,
Buddha would be the flashpoint for an argument (which
you wouldn't start) and, who knows, even a definitive
separation. And then, with a clairvoyant lucidity that
frightened you like the intrepid lane change of a suicidal
motorcyclist, you saw yourself living with the dog alone.
You would take him out to walk two times a day. You
would buy him the best food. You would give him a special corner of your rented apartment, small, hermitage-like
(without a nativity scene, framed photos, or too much
polish on the floor). You would take him to the vet and
the dog groomer. And Buddha and you both would look
harmonious, fully inured to your respective new lives.

THE 9/11 STORY NOBODY
ASKED ME TO WRITE

Memory has little to do with the things we've lived through.
In real time, the horror and weight of the images grow, as
if wanting to wallow in their status as the most significant
terrorist attack in history. At first—at lunchtime on a
Tuesday, a holiday, when it is still our time zone, and not
New York's, that matters—there's nothing but a prelude,
announced with an indifference that will soon collapse,
like the first tower itself. Concentric filters of information
impose their hierarchy: New York, Madrid, Barcelona.
New York for obvious reasons; Madrid, for a journalistic
response that grasps the magnitude of the tragedy; and
Barcelona because of the particular details of a regional
holiday, September 11, and a coffee drunk when what you
really want to do is take a nap. Our children are still little
and seem to have negotiated some kind of cease-fire. Soon

they realize the television has gripped us with unfamiliar magnetism. Instinctively, they don't interrupt our terror or our stupefaction as adults rarely interested in current affairs. By now, channel surfing is a reflex of the person hungry for information. And for a few minutes, which it will take me fifteen years to assimilate, my brain secretes a kind of toxic adrenaline. I recognize it: it's the adrenaline of panic. It tends to flood me at inopportune times, and I've learned to tame it by breathing slowly and applying a rigorous protocol. It's simple and requires more discipline than willpower. It consists of negating or deemphasizing the possible causes of panic, clinging to things as they are, and fleeing all interpretation. We are now more than a few years into my life as a father, and as news comes of people jumping from flaming windows in the first tower, I try to find analogues to my panic on my mind's hard drive. There are none. The sequence of events compels me to put in an earphone. Connected to the radio, I don't lose my good manners, and I exchange comments with Anna in monosyllables. Fifteen years have gone by and we've never talked about it, about that afternoon, since (in fact, we've never talked about anything from our past since), but I remember—or I think I do—the way she quickly grasped the scope of the event. She fell prey neither to exhibitionistic terror nor to what we now call *empathy* and used to call *compassion* or *pity*. When the tower fell, I noticed her spontaneous urge to

The 9/11 Story Nobody Asked Me to Write

cry, which was different from my more hysterical and, let's say, *cultural* one. The special broadcasts on the radio and television came together in an all-consuming fever of consternation that continues to burn and feeds on everything that has been swept away since. Neither our children nor we are what we might have been if the attack had never occurred. That is the justification for reexamining archives, clippings, film, and testimony from those days, undergoing a mental regression or ersatz psychotherapy, and focusing on what I did, felt, and thought, dividing that unprecedented day from the more routine sequence of my life. We know almost everything about the major figures in the tragedy, but what interests me is to contrast that with the peculiar microcosm of a well-to-do home in Barcelona and the microscopic emotion— in comparison with the angst of the world in aggregate—provoked in us by the disappearance of not one, but now both skyscrapers. As always, when she tries, Anna finds the proper tone, and though it isn't especially apposite, she recollects aloud the day in August 1994 when we went up to the observatory of the Twin Towers, how happy we were to be there but how disappointed we were by the safety windows and the massive herd of tourists we were part of. Soon, from panic, I remove myself from this circuit, which is in reality the circuit of those privileged enough to be elsewhere, free to think of the pain it relieves me not to have to share, but which I can't

consider wholly alien, either. With one part of my brain
connected to the radio, I gather information. I interiorize
the sounds of secondary explosions, of murder, presum-
ably, and confused announcements of presidents sheltered
in bunkers preparing for nuclear war, and all the
alarms—I mean all of them—going off. The reaction I
expect from myself is the usual one: cowardice. But the
situation is exceptional enough to invite the possibility of
surprise. The foreseeable resort to tachycardia or fainting
isn't yet on the horizon. And I have the sense that I might
profit from the space separating the imminence of events
from events themselves to build a mental firewall between the towers and myself. To do so, I turn my attention to a single, monstrously selfish, but effective goal:
thinking of how we ourselves might be affected by the
appearance of chaos in the world, which the images are
transforming into a kind of behind-the-scenes simulation
of the apocalypse. Overlooking the planetary significance
of what's happening, I transform my son into the epicen-
ter of history. Which he was as soon as he was born. Despite preliminary tensions during the pregnancy, which I
aggravated with my pointless distress, everything turned
out (apparently) fine. Three days later, they diagnosed
him with complications that changed the rotation of the
universe. I didn't hesitate to show my true self. When the
doctor gave us the diagnosis, I collapsed from a combined
attack of tachycardia and lipothymia. A few minutes later,

stretched out on a gurney, I realized that this time, the resort to escapism—fainting is an organic form of escape—would resolve nothing, and that one way or another, I'd have to roll up my sleeves and imitate those people who do all that they can without knowing where their limits lie. And so, without an instruction manual, I pledged myself to a half-Japanese, half-Soviet ethic of responsibility. That was my weapon, and for what it was worth, it served me until the day when two airplanes, hijacked by Islamist terrorists, destroyed the Twin Towers in New York and forever interrupted the lives of much of the planet's population. My memory is selective, and combines the telegenic solemnity of Matías Prats on Antena 3 with the adaptive intuition of Gaspar Hernàndez of Catalunya Radio. As soon as they come on, the eyewitness testimony functions as an emotional airbag. Whoever is talking has survived and, like a science fiction movie alien, will regrow their tentacles while making a rough assessment of the damage. But in the minuscule space between the sofa and the TV, with our children toying with Lego pieces, I no longer think of the victims in New York or their mayor's courage or the historic and journalistic import of the images of people who appear, like an army of zombies before zombies were back in fashion, walking amid clouds of dust from fires, crushed concrete, and hate. My world contracts to fortify me, and I focus on what I have to do, to

keep what's happening—my panic prevents me from
imagining its dimensions, but for that very reason, I
realize they must be unimaginable—from being so horrible for me, and *me* here signifies myself and my children. I make a series of pedestrian calculations. Of all
the possible consequences, I overlook the most probable:
financial collapse, military escalation, stock market
crashes and sectarian reprisals, and decide I must act
instead of thinking. Act while thinking of myself, that
is, which means thinking of my son and the possibility
that, as a minor, derivative consequence of the disaster,
pharmacies won't receive their shipments of medicine
and the law of the jungle will prevail over supply and
demand. It was as if I could see it: lines, riots, black
market, contraband, looting. This thought endues me
with an almost robotic energy. I change clothes, put on
my shoes, and walk outside to withdraw as much money
as I can from the ATM and—especially—to buy the
maximum number of boxes of the antibiotic my son's
chronic ailment obliges him to take in variable doses,
depending on how he feels. In the meantime, the towers
are history, because they've fallen and not because they
were built. For that reason, perhaps, they give rise to
paradigm changes and changes in language, alter hu-
manistic constellations, and annihilate thousand-year-
old religious certainties. The fire has overtaken
everything, but I restrict myself, compress myself into

the task I have set. It's a holiday in Barcelona and I have to go from one twenty-four-hour pharmacy to another. Luckily, we live in a country where the need for a prescription remains providentially arbitrary, and over time, I've developed a foolproof technique for getting antibiotics without dealing with the bureaucracy: I talk about my sick child, inventing a pediatrician who's left town and has given me the prescription urgently over the phone. Almost always—one day, I'll have to buy dinner for every pharmacist in the city—they respond with discretion and decency and just the right measure of pliability. My haul: seventeen boxes of antibiotics, which assure me a two to three months' supply, and I calculate—without any special rigor—that this is how long whatever began at nine a.m. local time will last— our new local time, since our old one—three, four, five, six, seven, eight, nine p.m.—no longer has any meaning, and already they're announcing military strikes, extraordinary sessions of the Security Council, the simultaneous closure of Wall Street and airspace. My own airspace has already been closed for some time now. I am wandering through my personal sewers, on my private mission to gather antibiotics, repeating and perfecting the story that allows me to go from pharmacy to pharmacy and get them sans prescription, paying with cash I've withdrawn from the machine, permanently hooked up to the radio. The radio, so useful, so precise, so imperative to feed the outpouring of a panic that seems to diminish with each new box of antibiotics acquired. As though there existed a direct relation between pure, universal panic and my own apprehension, so irrelevant, so specific, so selfish, and yet so real.

FATHER–SON
CHRISTMAS CAROL

Nostalgia is archaeology: it looks for vestiges and interprets them. But instead of applying the scientific method, it draws on the tendentious mechanics of memory. To speak of the effects of learning that Santa Claus is your parents, which is what you've proposed to do, you must situate yourself in a faraway moment of your childhood. You remember: they raised you in mystery, told to never ask questions and to trust your surroundings as a matter of course. Making your way through the stages of a happy childhood, you developed your own interpretation of the world, all the while remaining obedient to your family. The margin of interpretation this opened up led you to believe a number of absurdities, such as that, if you wrote a letter with a list of your favorite toys, a fat bearded man in a red uniform would climb down the chimney (that you didn't have) on the night between December 24 and 25. As in most familial autarkies, the secret to the story was its plausibility, the conviction of those who expounded it, and the collaboration of those who conserved the lie in the name of the magic of Christmas and with the pretext of tradition. It's true that now and again, at school or on the street, older children would come over and whisper the hidden truth in your ear. But the weight of the majority and your parents' authority prevailed, and the sole effect of those more malign versions of the tale was to open incidental cracks in the edifice of the truth. From the archaeological point of view, nostalgia may transform an unpleasant reality into a symptom of a civilization that manages to hold on to its myths, establishing a clear distinction between children and adults in terms of their access to fiction. But for the lie to work, adults have to play their part. And for reasons that escape you, your father transgressed the norm—he must have agreed with your mother that the time had come to abandon, like diapers, the infantile habit of believing in Santa Claus— and, three days before the holiday, taking advantage of a spell at home after one of his many absences (absences you dealt with, naturally, by not asking questions), he announced the two of you would go look at toys at the Le Printemps department store. The announcement was as sober as it was spectacular. He didn't include any concrete details, but the excursion was still a change from the

traditional method of writing a list. And the key words
were *look at*. You remember this outing, perhaps because you and your father made very few of them alone.
You do suspect that memory has intervened to magnify
its relevance; and that, like the archaeologist thrilled by
the find of a tarnished sestertius in an excavation, you
exaggerate its numismatic significance. You remember:
it was a long walk from your home to the center of Paris,
then an hour more by bus and metro. You must have
been six or seven, and you held your father's gigantic
hand with the intention—and following your mother's
insistently repeated commandment—of not letting him
go under any circumstances. Your father wasn't a man of
many words, but he knew how to inhabit a reassuring
silence, and just when you began to suspect there was
something strange in his going so long without speaking,
he would smile and utter some idle phrase to lasting
effect, for example: *What a pain life is!* This is the secret
of the taciturn: every word they speak rises to the cate-
gory of the memorable. Viewed from a distance, you
allow yourself to suspect this jaunt was the result of an
ultimatum imposed by your mother: *The kid hasn't seen
you for months. Either you take him out or you can pack
your bags,* she must have said—your mother was always
comfortable with ultimatums, perhaps because they were
the only tactic that worked with your father. Discomfited,
he must have viewed it as a mission, a compulsory

adventure that obliged him, for the first time in years, to submit to such extravagancies as buying two bus tickets, making sure his young son didn't stray or cause some problem with unimaginable consequences (particularly for an exile living in hiding with false papers), and offering him, more or less, a bit of conversation. More attentive to the rituals of clandestinity than to those of fatherhood, he paused now and again to be sure no one was following us, and when he saw nothing untoward, you went down to catch the metro. You loved the metro, especially that sequence of gigantic illustrations pasted on the walls of the tunnel: an ad for Dubonnet divided into three panels. The first, which you discovered with your nose pressed to the glass just when the cars set in motion, showed a man in a chair, preparing to drink from his glass of wine, and the liquid filled, as if he himself were a bottle, a small part of his body. Below him were the letters DUBO. A few moments later, still traveling slowly, the second panel appeared, with the man now drinking from the glass and even more alcohol rising in his body. And at last, in the third image, the burgundy color of the wine soaked the man completely, yet he poured himself still another glass, enlivened by the now concluded text: DUBO, DUBON, DUBONNET. You emerged in a station downtown; it was already dark when you set foot on the Boulevard Hausmann, and the surroundings held a profusion of stimuli you had never come across before. Used to the outskirts, where the tribe detected anything with the whiff of novelty right away, the monumental boulevard, luxurious and overrun with the Christmas swarms, was a spectacle that compelled you and your father to hold hands even tighter than before. You had been to this department store before, but never at this time of year. Decorated with a pharaoh's sense of spectacle, the façade featured constellations of lights meant to beguile the multitudes. At every door of the building, on every floor and beside every escalator, there was a man disguised as Santa Claus with instructions to smile and wave to the customers, especially the children. Each could detect your vulnerability to being dazzled, and each followed the company policy of cordiality with the same discipline with which you responded to their overtures. Cutting a path through the waves of consumption, you arrived at the toy department, uncertain how to take in so much temptation. And aware, perhaps, that all that stimulus was overwhelming you, your father revealed the true purpose of the expedition: "Take a look at everything, and when we go home and you write your letter, say which toy you like best." You grasped this proposal immediately, being schooled in the revolutionary discipline of obedience and not the frustration of bourgeois cravings. And you let yourself be carried along and looked greedily at all these discoveries, guessing which ones were there only to be admired (electric trains, Scalextric racetracks, and other inaccessible capitalist pastimes) and which might get past your mother's censure, being feasible and, so to speak, proletarian. And maybe that was when you first came to feel the tiny cracks in the marble surface of the truth widening into an irreparable hemorrhage; or else, without knowing how to define it—you had neither the vocabulary nor the awareness to do so—you felt a justifiable hint of distrust. You didn't let the opportunity pass. Instinctively, you tied up all the loose ends you had left to lie from pure credulity and uttered the fateful question: "Why are there so many Santa Clauses at all the doors and on every floor if there's only one Santa Claus?" If today, fifty years later, a group of archaeologists were to study your father's face just then—after donning their latex gloves, lifting it gently with tweezers, and cleaning the dust off with a camel's hair brush—they would authenticate it as an expression of panic and resignation. Panic at not knowing what to say, and resignation at not having foreseen, when my mother had his back against the wall, that the thing that was now happening to him— against his will—might happen. And then, to demonstrate that fatherhood is ninety percent improvisation and ten percent panic, he knelt down, as if on the verge of revealing the definitive truth. First he resorted to the universal paternal gesture: mussing his son's hair with his hand and smiling with apparent complicity. It's an ancestral stalling tactic for adults looking for a response that

will permit them to evade their child's interrogatory
ambush. And as he affectionately mussed your hair, his
eyes swept quickly over the room. With the agility of a
toreador who knows in a tenth of a second he will have to
dodge a wounded and infuriated beast, he avoided an-
swering (or maybe it would be best to say he avoided the
question) with the same virtues Jacinto Benavente attributed to Joselito: delicacy, agility, skill, speed, ease,
flexibility, and grace. Instead, he pointed toward a toy
that stood out as though someone had placed it there for
the sole purpose of your falling in love with it, with one of
those deft sweeps of the cape that throws a charging bull
off course. A child's love is as fickle as it is portentous.
But, perhaps because your father knew what to do to keep
you from delving too deep into the mystery of the multi-
ple Santa Clauses, an air gun appeared before you, one that
shot little pellets at plastic silhouettes with numbers
printed on them. When the pellets hit the heart of the sil-
houette, it would fall down and the shooter would rack up
points. The toy's price must have conformed to whatever
dictates were imposed in advance, because when, a few
days later, you and your brother ran down to the foot of the
Christmas tree to see what Santa Claus had brought, you
tore impatiently into the wrapping paper (coincidentally,
from Le Printemps) and found, in a perfect little package,
the air pistol, the kit with the collapsing silhouettes, and
two cartridges of pellets. The toy kept you entertained for

months while—without wheedling from others, when you managed to take shelter in your private, inner monologues—you arrived at the conclusion that if you go to a department store and there are dozens of Santa Clauses and you can see their false beards and their breath stinks of Dubonnet, that maybe the wicked older kids from the neighborhood were right when they came over and whispered the Truth in your ear. And from that day forward, every time you took aim at the colorful silhouettes (which fell more and more precariously), you would imagine them as a platoon of bogus Santas, vestiges of a childhood archaeologically surmounted.

POETICS

You were out of propranolol tablets, and you went to the neighborhood pharmacy, which never closes, to buy a box. You're a regular customer, and you paid with a fifty-euro bill. You put the change in your pocket without bothering to count it, took two pills, and entered the Pakistani convenience store on the corner to refill your stock of water and Coke Zero. You call it *the Pakistani convenience store on the corner* though it's not on the corner, but in the middle of the block, between a beauty parlor run by a compulsive smoker and the office of an electrician who resembles General Custer. The Pakistani store opened recently and is overseen by a man a bit younger and fatter than you. His television is permanently tuned to a channel that alternates between furious imams, noisy game shows, and cricket matches, and in the cooler, he has yogurts in flavors you can find

nowhere else. To pay, you removed a twenty-euro bill
(from the change from the pharmacy), but when the clerk
took it from your hand, he immediately told you, "It's
fake." At first, you felt embarrassed, particularly given
the severity of his tone, as if he thought you were trying
to pawn off a counterfeit bill. All you could think of was
to babble a disjointed apology and take out another bill in
the hope it wasn't false. It wasn't. Water and Coca-Cola
in hand, you returned home feeling vulnerable and dis-
turbed. You considered going back to the pharmacy and
demanding they change the bill. But you hazarded that
the people from the pharmacy, who haven't asked you to
see a prescription in years, would feel bad if you accused
them of passing you a fake bill (a bill that, in fact, no one
can verify that they gave you, because you should have
checked it at the moment when they broke the fifty). And,
activating your compensatory mechanism, you arrived at
the conclusion that, precisely because it is an ambivalent
situation, it might have the makings of an article (taking
the anecdote as a metaphor for everything, like a medical
analysis of a tiny sample of blood that elucidates the past,
present, and future of a thriving or moribund organ-
ism). The antagonistic forces that collided in your brain
were (a) worry that the Pakistani shopkeeper—who, for
the purposes of the article, could just as well be Indian,
Afghani, or Iranian—might think you meant to swindle
him because he was a new arrival in the country, and

interpret this as a racist or colonial reflex; (b) fear that the pharmacist would feel unjustly accused of trafficking in false currency, and would stop being so gentle and efficient (even turning a blind eye when you ask for the antidepressants you self-medicate with); and (c) which is the worst part, far and away—your unwillingness to admit that in any awkward situation, instead of acting naturally and taking things as they are, your tactics are inevitably subdued, paranoid, and insecure, and if you had to sum them up with a single adjective, a motto for the author of the present article, which you probably still won't dare to write, you would undoubtedly choose the word *craven*.

BONUS TRACK

You will realize, when you're about to finish the manuscript that you've been writing for five years, that deep down, all you've done is ruminate on the idea that you were unable to make another person happy. *Truly make another person happy,* you will write, to emphasize the affirmation's finality. Eluding the allure of self-pity, you will remember that you did make your parents and brothers happy, especially when you were little and you exuded a joy that made you, putting modesty aside, a good companion. Later, without meaning to, you began to specialize in creating situations that would make others happy. From inertia or ineptitude, you never became the main provider of a kind of happiness that could withstand questioning the reasons for so much enthusiasm and commitment. You subjugated your children to an unconditional love that smothered them and solved thousands of problems (even problems they didn't have) and foresaw catastrophes you avoided with sterile discipline. Lord of the Castle of What If, you practiced the feudalism of overprotectiveness, ever attentive to what could contribute to the hypothetical happiness of your descendants, who were half serf and half puppy. This was happiness—or rather, comfort taken to its furthest extreme—but you never managed to share it, because when your children were with you, they were safe and invulnerable but also tense from the responsibility of living up to demands you created with the excuse of love and protectiveness at a time when they were free from expectations but, at the same time, expected to be everything. Then you realized it wasn't too late, but circumstances placed you between the devil (no longer doing what was easiest) and the deep blue sea (vulnerability to the risks that growing brings with it).

And Anna? you ask yourself, just to confirm that writing her name doesn't upset you. As in every good movie, the two of you were in New York. You'd decided to have a child not long before. You had never been so happy. It was evident in your way of being: intense and excessive, vexatious and demanding, attentive and meticulous. It was evident when you laughed during the day, in the way you walked, in the way you looked at her and listened to her, even when you thought she was being too quiet and you had to bite your tongue to respect her silences. It was evident when you tried Indian food or when you talked, with the smugness of a jazz expert, about the same Abdullah Ibrahim that she had just turned you on to. You went to the Tower Records on Broadway and got her a Jimmy Durante CD with, among others, the song "Make Someone Happy." And since you had arrived at the furthest imaginable reaches of comfort, you decided to be unusually spontaneous and bought a combo radio–CD player in an electronics store in the neighborhood overseen by a couple from Surinam. And with that invasive impatience you used to confuse with graciousness, you insisted on bringing it out in the apartment a friend—of Anna's—had let you use. No one has ever let *you* use their apartment, not in New York or anywhere else. And there, with the windows open, with the views of the adjacent buildings, in ignorance of just how fulfilled you were, you made her listen, not worrying whether she would like it or not, to that song that insisted you should make someone happy, make just one someone happy, that was the whole point of existence. With Durante singing it, everything seemed simple. But now that you're about to finish the manuscript, you can be certain, without a single trace of remorse, that you couldn't manage it, because perfectionism, reason, and logic interfered, a possessive fear of everything, a godforsaken presumption of integrity that poisoned it all. At the time, that possibility was only the embryonic specter of a hypothesis that you rejected with the arrogance of a man in love, because

117

you had all the energy in the world. Then, as the years passed, and circumstances imposed a need for balance, you convinced yourself that whereas your love, at one time, had been generously requited, your happiness—now it no longer hurts to call it that, because you know the countdown is coming to an end—was always subordinate to whatever was most convenient, prudent, or—worst of all—urgent. And as you notice, more relieved than depressed, that the end of the book is imminent, and the fear swells in your stomach because you don't know what will come afterward, when you're sure that it's over, you ask yourself whether you'll faint, the way Jaume Cabré does, or so they say, every time he finishes a manuscript. And at the same time, you have the feeling, perhaps, that you've taken too long to reach the heart of the question embodied in a song from a musical that changes so much depending on who's singing and the mood of the person listening.

For you, the only version will be Jimmy Durante's, in New York in the summer of 1994. With Anna's summer freckles and a dress with a Provençal print. With her generosity in taking you in like a piece of furniture found on the sidewalk, of keeping up the joke that you were like the dogs in *Lady and the Tramp*. Her, pretty as a princess; you, a mutt, but without the charm and audacity of Disney's animated orphans. Like the tramp from the film, you and the lady shared your plate of spaghetti, but, to

Bonus Track

stick to the song's one and only message, you didn't know how to make her happy. You knew how to love her, how to be where you had to be, how to commit. But never with that touch of arbitrary pyrotechnics that distinguishes the men who stick in your mind—who say yes when someone tells them no, who drive with one hand and don't get scared when they have to sign a mortgage, who tell a tax inspector to cool his jets, or book a trip to Istanbul—from men who are merely necessary. For you, "Make Someone Happy" will always be the Jimmy Durante version, because in just two minutes, he wraps things up with the optimism of a man who's seen it all and lays out perfectly the idea of priorities. Despite everything. Despite everyone. Make someone happy. Make just one someone happy. That's what life is about, reduced to its maximally minimum expression. And you will think how it's not worth mentioning that over recent years you assembled, almost on the sly, different versions of the song, including the one by Jamie Cullum. And that you listened to the last of these on repeat on your iPod while walking with no other object than to burn enough calories to counter—exercise being one of the pillars of your treatment—the diabetes they've just diagnosed you with. And that you are aware that this rendition is too intense, but still majestic, and as addictive as adding more adjectives and adverbs than are pertinent when you write. And you often felt the temptation to wallow in a grief imposed

by the culture that loves pain, made worse by the drama
of absences we ourselves are responsible for—because,
in an example of prosaic justice, the consequence of not
knowing how to make someone happy is solitude, you
told yourself. And without bothering to note whether it
made you feel better or worse, you listened to it over and
over again. Make someone happy, make just one someone
happy, Cullum repeated with ideal raspiness, in contrast
with Durante's optimistic maturity. And again—because
there's still room in the margins—you will realize that
Durante was a match for the way you were then: impatient, excessive, pyrotechnic, sentimental, joyous, when
you wanted to have a child and didn't know you'd have
three. When Anna still looked at you with a blend of curiosity and eagerness, of respect and benevolence (never of
passion: a man can't have it all). Whereas Cullum likely
corresponds more with how you feel now: vulnerable,
contradictory, and insecure, convinced she will always be
the best thing that ever happened to you but you'll never
be the best thing that happened to her. And you've never
told anyone, not Anna, not your kids, who made you so
happy, and you've gone on gathering different versions
of the song, and sometimes, even those of Judy Garland
or Barbra Streisand tempt you. And inevitably—and not
even today will be an exception—you returned to that lu-
minous window in an apartment in New York, when you
watched how Anna smiled and acknowledged you with

an expression that—you finally realize now—meant that she still hoped you would make her happy and that, day after day—and through the course of many years—she would give you—you and no one else—the opportunity to be the one who did it.